CATCHING
— THE —
LAST TRAM

SUSAN HOLT

INLET PUBLISHING

FREE DOWNLOAD

Sign up for the author's New Releases mailing list
and get a free short story.

Go here to get started: susanholt.nz/free

ABOUT THE AUTHOR

Susan Holt lives in New Zealand. She believes
stories can change the world and is doing her very
best to make this a change for the better.

Find out more at susanholt.nz

ISBN 978-0-473-39510-0

A catalogue record for this book is available from the National Library
of New Zealand.

Editing: Michelle Elvy
Layout and design: Tessa Baty

Published by Inlet Publishing, susanholt.nz

It never would have happened without you,
my incredible Robert. Thank you!

—— ONE ——

"You have got to be kidding me."

Beth turned to the man, who was still muttering under his breath. They'd been waiting for ten minutes in the dazzling morning sun, but he hadn't spoken before. Every few minutes someone else had ambled up and silently stationed themselves around about the bus stop. Quite a number of them stood there now, suits and skirts highly pressed, all ignoring each other.

He seemed to have been reacting to something at the top of the road. Beth turned to see the bus had appeared in the distance. But she had never seen a bus like it in all her time living in this city.

It was old, yes. But there was something about it more peculiar than old. It was as if it didn't quite fit in the world, like a black and white photograph pasted onto a science fiction movie poster.

She liked it immediately. It was, in fact, a tram, its single wand extending from the roof up to the overhead line. The tram ran along a set of rails running flush with the road top. She hadn't noticed either the tracks or the overhead line before.

Most of its frame was wood, the panels green and yellow with the number 17 stencilled on the front. It was in good condition. No rust, no peeling paint.

As the tram approached the group at the stop, Beth heard everyone around her begin to complain. They shook their heads and heaved great sighs and clicked their tongues as they rolled their eyes.

"Lord, I hope this is the only time we have to get this one," grumbled a woman nearby.

Beth asked, "Why? What's wrong with it?"

The woman looked at her as if she was stupid. "It'll only take forever." Then she went back to ignoring Beth.

As the tram got closer, Beth could hear the zing of the connection drawing power from the mains. The pitch lowered as the tram slowed down and stopped next to the bus stop sign—right in front of Beth.

The door clacked open and Beth lifted her foot to step up. But some schoolboys appeared out of nowhere and shoved her out of the way. The boys stomped up the stairs, flashing their passes at the driver.

Regaining her balance, Beth found herself competing with the rest of the small crowd as they pressed in to get their seats. She let them go ahead. She was paying by cash, after all. That took time and she didn't want anyone behind her to get annoyed.

Finally she stepped up to the driver. "I haven't used this route before. How much to the city, please?"

The driver had a friendly face, his cheeks ruddy as he welcomed her on board. "Ah, of course. You're new to the area?" He pressed a few metal keys and the fare amount clicked up onto the manual readout.

It was nice to meet a driver willing to chat. She grinned

back. "Yes. Moved in Saturday. Nice and close to the bus stop." She fished around in her purse for the correct change.

When she pulled her hand out she found the usual mix of coins and lint plus an odd-looking coin she'd never seen before. Its surface was rough and she couldn't even see what denomination it was. She shrugged and held it up to the driver.

"Hey, look at this: funny money. Do you collect coins?"

The driver's bright expression broadened even further. "Oh, that's the good stuff. Yes, we take those." He took Beth's fare—including the old coin—and gave her a ticket.

Well! Goodness me!

Out of the corner of her eye, she saw a few of the passengers check their watches and shake their heads impatiently. She thanked the driver, closed her purse and made her way down the aisle to look for a seat.

She slipped into one near the back, behind the rear door, next to a dark-haired, slim man who was staring out the window. She was pleasantly surprised to find the driver waited until she sat down before he drove off. He rang the bell twice—*clang clang!*—as the tram got underway. She hoped he was always the driver on this route. He'd made her day already.

There'd been a fair few people at Beth's stop, but they hadn't filled the tram; no one was standing up yet. There'd been a handful of people on board already. Hers must be one of the first stops on the route.

She took in the interior. As with the exterior, it was mostly wood, with wooden poles lining the aisle. Hanging from the ceiling was a double row of long leather loops to hold on to. The floor was a set of strips running the length of the tram, leaving grooves in between. This type of floor would be a problem for women in stilettos.

Two long lengths of what looked like leather were threaded sideways through eyelets positioned above the windows. One on each side. To get off, you pulled down on a cord which alerted the driver by ringing one of the two bells on the ceiling above him.

The tram was beautiful. It had none of the sterile bars and plastic buttons of the newer diesel buses. The upholstery was plain and simple, but comfortable. The ceiling and the walls above the main windows were painted with silver and black swirling patterns. The fittings were made of brass.

It did rattle a bit and a breeze blew through certain holes around the doors and windows, but the tram rumbled soothingly along. No engine throbbed under them. They simply glided from stop to stop.

The man next to her was uninterested in talking. He sat erect, his gaze angled out the window. He appeared to be quite lost in thought.

In fact, no one spoke. They were all too tired, perhaps. Monday morning was never a good time to insist on a conversation. Never mind. Perhaps on the way home.

As the tram rolled along, the interior filled more and more and the new patrons had to stand. A middle-aged businesswoman with a large briefcase and another bag over her shoulder stopped right alongside Beth.

She looked up at the woman. "Would..."

But she was interrupted.

"Please, have a seat." The man next to the window leapt up as he spoke. Beth shuffled herself over to the window but couldn't believe it when she saw the woman sneer at the man as she sat down. He didn't notice and moved towards the rear.

The woman leaned in to Beth and whispered, "Sexist machismo!" She shook her head.

Beth remained silent. Standing up to help another wasn't

sexist. To her, it was merely the right thing to do. In fact, she'd been about to offer the woman her own seat. She wondered what kind of response she would've got.

The woman got a sheaf of papers out of her bag and proceeded to pore over them as if she was studying for an exam.

Beth looked out the window. They were crossing the bridge. She watched as two ferries passed each other going the opposite way.

When she turned back, an elderly woman was standing in the aisle next to the back door. Beth couldn't believe no one had offered her a seat. Shaking her head, she stood and excused herself to the businesswoman. "Sorry, may I get out?"

The woman huffed at her and pulled her papers out of the way. Beth was forced to step right over her briefcase before the woman shoved it towards the window, slid over and returned to her papers.

Beth spoke to the elderly woman. "Please, take my seat."

The lady beamed up at her—she was rather short—and said, "Oh, thank you, dear!" She eased herself down into the seat.

Beth smiled to herself.

From further down the tram, behind an enormous man in a bowtie, Beth could now see the man she'd been sitting next to before. He was smiling at her, she wasn't sure why. But she smiled back anyway.

As they reached the city, people began to get off, including Mr Bowtie. Beth found herself now standing next to her old seat-mate. He wasn't overly tall, but he was neatly dressed in a tailored camel-coloured tweed suit over a soft white shirt. His hair was short back and sides, though it had a slight hint of careful styling, the fringe curving neatly to one side.

He seemed more open to conversation now, and regarded

her in a friendly way, so she said hello.

His blue eyes crinkled. "Good morning." He smiled. His voice was deep and smooth.

"You usually catch this?" she asked.

"Every day."

"What kind of work do you do?" she asked.

The question made him pause, which surprised Beth—most men had a ready answer for questions about their careers.

"I… take care of people."

Are you being cagey?

"Management? Counselling?" she fished.

He smirked and nodded. "Management."

This was harder than usual. Perhaps he was a very private man.

"You?" he prompted her.

"I'm a librarian."

His eyes widened and he gasped. "Ah, wonderful! Libraries are extraordinary places."

She blinked at him. "Well yes, they are. But I've not often heard it expressed so enthusiastically."

He actually seemed just as enamoured of libraries as she was. How refreshing.

"Ha! I don't know why." He raised his eyebrows and added, "Where else can you visit all the countries of the world, find out the thoughts of the man next to you and what pygmy elephants have for breakfast, all in the one place?"

The way he put this made her giggle. Pygmy elephants? It reminded her of the times she'd bored—or horrified—various friends with her research on venomous snakes or lethal gases or water crystals or… so many other things.

"Well, yes. I agree," she replied. "But too many people don't see it like that. "You go there a lot?"

His face dropped. "Ah, no, unfortunately. I can never get there."

For a brief moment, Beth thought she'd caught him out, but he looked truly sad, so she forgave him instantly.

And then she noticed how many stops had passed while she'd been thinking of pygmy elephants and water crystals. "Oh, heavens. We've gone past my stop."

The man chuckled, leaned over and pulled the cord for her.

"Thank you," she said as they coasted to a halt. "Perhaps I'll see you tomorrow."

"Perhaps," he replied, and smiled stiffly.

She sensed he was withdrawing from her.

Perhaps not.

The back door clacked open and she descended the stairs, calling out to the driver, "Thank you!"

He waved to her through the rear vision mirror attached to the front window. "Cheerio!"

What a lovely driver.

As she walked back to the last stop, she checked her watch. She was in good time for work. Early even. What had those people at the stop been moaning about?

— TWO —

Invigorated by her fellow passenger's zeal about her workplace, Beth spoke with added fervour to the school groups visiting that day. She told them all about the "wonders of the library." She even managed to mention pygmy elephants, which elicited a giggle from the little ones on the mat.

"You don't believe me, do you? But you never know what you're going to come across in this place. Just behind that shelf there…" She pointed, bringing her voice down to a whisper, "is a sabre-toothed tiger."

A girl down the back let out a little excited scream.

"And over the other side of the lending desk is where all the snakes live."

The boys in particular were lapping it up, their wide eyes drinking it all in, little grins on their faces.

They'll be back.

At lunchtime, Ruby, her boss, asked how the move had gone over the weekend and mentioned that Beth had her annual job appraisal next week. Beth hoped she would get a raise; it was about time.

Her new flatmate, Jay, gave Beth a lift home in her car. Jay had been delivering artworks to the far side of the city, and they'd arranged the ride earlier that morning. It was convenient to travel door-to-door by car, and it saved her a little money, but really Beth would've preferred to have used public transport. A squall of rain hit, which made visibility difficult and the pockets of angry drivers, aggressively cutting in, tooting their horns and gesticulating at each other's behaviour, was nerve-wracking. At least in a bus you were a little removed from it.

But the two young women chatted amicably all the way home, and Beth found herself describing her ride in the tram that morning in great detail.

"Well, well, well," said Jay, when Beth had finished. "So, how old was he?"

Beth frowned. "Oh, I dunno. Maybe late forties, perhaps fifty-something. He kind of looked like Santa, but in a big blue coat and hat."

"But you said he was thin." Jay seemed taken aback.

Beth stared at her, mouth open, until she figured out where she'd gone wrong. "Oh, no, I was talking about the driver."

"Why?"

"You asked about him."

This was true, as the driver had been the last person she'd been talking about, and he'd made quite a happy impression.

Jay sighed and rolled her eyes. "I was asking about the dark, handsome one, you silly woman. Do you think you'll talk to him again?" They were sitting at a traffic light and Jay looked over her spectacles at Beth, her eyebrows raised. "I mean, he sounded… *hmmmm!*" The bright look in her eye made her meaning quite obvious.

Beth laughed and cleared her throat. Is that how she'd

come across, talking about this complete stranger? She hoped she hadn't been too forward with him.

"Oh, well, I don't know. He said he was on the tram every day."

Jay nudged her, grinning. "Great. It's a start."

The light went green and Jay returned to concentrating on the road. Beth didn't know how to respond. She hadn't been thinking about the man on the tram that way. Not yet.

Well… maybe.

He'd been pretty nice to look at, she had to admit, now she thought about it.

Oh dear.

Perhaps he'd thought she was flirting with him. Maybe that was why he'd pulled away at the end of their conversation.

Well, I'm going to feel uncomfortable around him now.

If she ever saw him again, he would probably run a mile. The same thing had happened with Dominic. She'd let the word 'relationship' pop out of her mouth too early and she'd never seen him again. And she suspected it might have been the case with Erich, too. She pinned all her hopes and dreams on whichever man was in front of her; they felt the weight of them, and ran for their lives.

"Damn," she murmured.

"What?" Jay was trying to negotiate a roundabout but was clearly still listening to Beth.

Come to think of it, Beth wouldn't have known how she was behaving if Jay hadn't pointed it out. Perhaps this time she could nip it in the bud.

Beth decided to confess. "Well, whenever I realise I'm attracted to someone, I behave strangely. I can never relax around them. It's frustrating."

"Why, do you think?"

"Oh, I'm nervous, I suppose," she said.

"What of?"

Beth paused, biting her lip. "I don't want to stuff it up, I guess. It's too important."

"Why so important?"

Beth felt her body become heavy. "Because I'm lonely," she admitted finally. "And I don't want to be alone for the rest of my life. I'd really like to be in love—and to be loved back."

"And how do you think you could stuff that up?" Jay asked.

Beth huffed and threw up her hands. "By being an idiot."

"You think being an idiot would put someone off?"

"Definitely!"

"What if being an idiot is part of who you are?"

Beth scoffed. "You mean unconditional idiocy?"

"Yes." Jay chuckled. "Kind of."

It was backwards and clumsy, but Beth could tell they understood each other. And it had lightened the mood, which was a relief.

She cracked up. "Well, there's got to be someone out there who can love an idiot, right?" she said.

"Yes, exactly," Jay said. "If they're not going to give you a second chance, they're not very forgiving, are they? Would you really want to be with someone like that?"

Beth shook her head, lips pursed. "Yeah, okay—no. But…" She wanted to get back to being serious again. "But what if they get the wrong impression of me?"

"Don't you think they're more likely to get the wrong impression of you if you're all tense and worried about what you're going to say, rather than comfortable with yourself and relaxed?"

"Yeah, I suppose," Beth admitted. "You mean, someone like me as *me*, rather than the person I'm *pretending* to be. I think I get you."

"Exactly. And besides," Jay added, "you can always apologise if you say something you didn't mean to."

Beth took a deep breath. "But that doesn't stop me from being nervous when I'm face-to-face with Mr Handsome. And that affects how I behave."

Jay sniggered. "Do you think, perhaps, you're worried about being too enthusiastic and letting him know you're attracted to him? Do you want to be cool, like: 'I don't care if you like me or not'? I'm not sure that's any more honest or caring. Why would you want him to think you're not interested in him?"

Yikes!

Jay had only known her a couple of weeks, but she could obviously see right through her.

But Beth knew the answer straight away. "I'm trying to protect myself."

"Right," said Jay. "Is that how you want to live? Curled up and safe—and alone?"

Wow! This girl doesn't hold out on her confrontations.

"No," Beth said. "No, I want to be myself and find out who'll like me for that."

Jay grinned. "You'll be surprised at how many there will be."

Beth beamed and ducked her head.

Good choice of flatmate.

—— THREE ——

So Beth was a mixture of pleased and nervous when she saw the tram gliding its way down the road towards her the next morning. She didn't care that all the people around her were peeved about the tram itself.

"What are they thinking? We travel the farthest, and they give us this thing?" The short man with flat feet shook his head, a sour expression on his face.

"I know. It doesn't make sense," said the woman with her arms crossed over her chest. "We should get the new ones, not the ones about to to break down."

"You mark my words: they'll end up making us push it!"

More tutting, more shaking of heads.

Beth withdrew from the bitter conversation and stared out over the shallow valley they were in as the tram coasted down the slope towards them. Roofs of various colours and shapes stretched away under the bright blue sky, trees dotted about the horizon.

The driver recognised her and greeted her with gusto, making her smile. She slid her coins—none of them antique this time—into the worn wooden bowl attached to the end of his cash-box.

She didn't have to look far to see Mr Handsome.

I really have to stop calling him that.

He was in the same seat as yesterday but this time he was watching her as she made her way down the aisle towards him, which made her heart miss a beat.

Someone else's eyes followed her too, one of the schoolboys who'd nearly knocked her flat yesterday. He was scowling.

Beth ignored the schoolboy and smiled as she sat down. "I hope you don't mind me joining you again."

"Not at all," the man replied, though his face showed a small frown for an instant before he looked down.

"I'm Beth, anyway. Hello." Beth held out her hand.

"Isaac. It's a pleasure to meet you." His tone was formal and he even bowed his head as he took her hand in his own and squeezed it—they had no room for their hands to shake in the normal manner as his arm was awkwardly jammed between them. Beth tried to give him a little more room, but the seats were small, and she couldn't go far.

She didn't mind that much.

A sudden explosion of laughter rolled forward from the back of the tram. It was the schoolboys and, though it wasn't obvious what they were laughing at, Isaac's face displayed another momentary frown.

Beth leaned towards him, indicated the boys with a flick of her eyes and murmured, "They almost bowled me over yesterday morning when I was trying to get on."

Isaac frowned. "Oh dear. I am sorry."

Beth smirked at him. "Why? Are they yours?"

He laughed. "No." He was very definite about it.

He was even more attractive when he smiled and her

stomach did a little flip-flop.

Yikes, girl, don't get ahead of yourself.

But she leapt straight in anyway. "So, why don't you go to the library, since you're so enamoured with the place?"

He sighed. "I can't get there, I'm afraid. I do love books and learning about different places and things. I miss it terribly." His eyes had a faraway look. "I spent many a happy hour browsing through the catalogue at my local library, when I was a young lad."

"You do know the library can deliver on demand, don't you?"

He looked at her with one eyebrow raised. "Really?"

"Oh, yes. If you look up the catalogue online, you can order a book via the internet."

His smile was self-mocking now. "Ah, yes, well. I don't get the internet," he explained.

Now it was Beth's turn to look at him askance. "You've got to be joking. You don't use the internet? At all?"

He raised his eyebrows and shook his head. "No. I deal with people."

But his eyes slid to the side for a second.

She stared at him, frowned, and then said, "You have a mobile, though, don't you?"

He looked at her blankly. "A mobile what?"

Beth was so taken aback—he must be joking—she laughed out loud, causing the woman across the aisle to glare at her. But they weren't in a library yet. And if the woman had heard what Isaac had just said…

But Beth stifled her giggle—for Isaac's sake—and drew out her smart phone, waggling it. "A mobile phone. You don't even use one for work?"

Surprisingly, he looked as though he had no idea what she was talking about. Perhaps he was unaccustomed to the new model—big screen, with her cheerful yellow case on it—because she could never *wear* yellow. So she unlocked her phone and showed him a few of the features: the music, the social media apps, the geography game.

He said nothing as he stared.

"And of course you can make a phone call." She paused. "Actually, it's a bit strange we still call it a phone. We don't use it for phone calls half as often as for everything else."

Hmmm! He smells so good.

Forcing her rebellious nose down to her phone, Beth opened the library app. "Let's find a book for you. What type of books do you like?" she asked.

He thought for a moment. "Hmmm. History?"

Beth clamped her lips together, trying not to laugh. "Um. You'll have to be more specific." She paused and then prompted him: "European history? Military history? Local history? Political history? Ancient history?"

His eyes widened and then blinked. "Recent history. The last century, perhaps. World history?"

Beth used the search facility and eighty six books came up, but then she remembered something.

"Actually, I know of a particular book you might like."

The benefits of talking to a librarian.

She grinned to herself as she flicked down the list. "Here it is," she said, and showed him the description.

"Oh yes, sounds fascinating." He seemed genuinely interested, but then he said, "Lots of people use these gadgets, don't they?" He was pointing at her phone. "I see them all the time, fiddling with them."

Gadgets?

Beth grinned at him, trying her best not to mock him too much. "You're kind of old-fashioned, aren't you?"

A flush crept up his cheeks. "You could say that, yes."

It all fitted: he was polite, a classic gentleman; his style of dress was conservative; he'd even referred to himself as a 'young lad' before. And his accent...

"Why is it 'phones' and not 'telephones' anymore, do you think?" he asked suddenly.

She raised her eyebrows. "Quicker, I suppose. Language tends towards more efficient use over time."

Well, look at that. I'm not acting like an idiot. I feel comfortable with him.

Then she had an idea. "Shall I set up a lending account for you? I can do it right now."

His eyes widened. "Really?"

"Absolutely." She selected the book and tapped 'Create account'. She felt happy to be useful to him, and sneaky too— this was one way to find out more about him.

"First name: Isaac. I-S-A-A-C?" She tried to act as professionally as possible. A professional librarian—was that a thing?

"Yes. Lyttelton." He spelled it for her and then paused. "Beth?"

"Yes?" She looked up.

"Short for Bethany?"

"Elizabeth," she admitted.

"Ah!" He smiled. "Elizabeth."

The way Isaac said her name made Beth feel warm. She bent her head down to the screen, in case she'd gone red.

"Address?" she asked, to cover her discomfort.

A long silence ensued. Beth felt the heat crawling up her neck, so she kept her head down until the silence was painful.

"What do you need an address for?" he asked, finally.

"I promise I won't stalk you." Beth grinned cheekily at him, trying to lighten the mood.

He looked at her, his face blank. "Stalk me?"

Perhaps the term wasn't in his vocabulary.

Beth chuckled. "Well, we have to have an address to send the book to."

"Ah," said Isaac. He tilted his head down and frowned. "Well, I'm not going to be able to give you an address, as a matter of fact." He looked away. "I didn't think of that. I apologise."

Beth didn't know how to react. Perhaps he thought she was creepy after all. But there could be another reason, so she would just wait and see. And hope.

Back off. Now.

She put her phone away.

"Oh well, that's a shame." She straightened in her seat and looked forward, trying to be nonchalant.

He seemed to sense a little of her disappointment, however. "Thank you for trying anyway," he said. "You're very thoughtful."

Beth smiled at her hands, bending her head further forward.

Oh dear! And it was going so well.

The tram came to a halt and a number of people got on. All the seats were full and a woman was standing in the aisle.

Isaac excused himself to Beth and stood up for the woman. At least it wasn't the businesswoman from yesterday, who might have scolded him for his generosity.

Once again, Beth shunted herself against the window, though she would have preferred to stay where she was, to be closer to Isaac. As it was, he walked right up the back anyway, so they couldn't even talk over the woman who'd sat down.

Beth's shoulders sagged. She must have pushed too much. He would probably never talk to her again now. He did seem to be holding himself back.

She should have checked whether he was married or not. She hadn't looked for a ring. It must be why he hadn't wanted to say where he lived. What a fool she was.

Beth's neck flamed up again and she faced the window, biting down on her lip. She felt angry with herself and a few tears of frustration were working their way down her cheeks; she didn't want anyone to see.

This is why they run away.

They were passing through a part of town she hadn't been through before. Well, she had—yesterday—but she obviously hadn't been looking out the window at the time. Everything she saw was new to her.

The road widened and the kerb of the road she was looking at merged into a flat, open space. They were moving into what looked like a large central depot. There were other trams there, sitting in various bays. But they were so far away Beth couldn't see if anyone was in them. In fact, the place looked deserted. Perhaps because it was so big.

The ground was crisscrossed with tracks going in all directions. The driver stopped at one point and opened the door. He got out and somehow the tram spun ninety degrees or so. From where she was sitting, Beth couldn't see the driver at all. Getting back on, he got them underway again, the door clacking back into place.

This fascinated Beth so much she forgot her embarrassment. If only she could go up and talk to the driver about what he was doing. There were too many people to push past right now, though. Perhaps she could do it another day.

That was a good idea. She would sit down the front tomorrow and prevent any more silliness with Isaac—the poor man. The driver was a good sort she would enjoy getting to know. And she wasn't attracted to him, so there wasn't any risk of her behaving like an idiot.

Right. No asking for his address. And don't laugh at him.

This plan in place, she felt a little easier and she watched as they passed suburb after suburb, all the time getting closer to the city.

After they crossed the bridge, people were getting off again and the tram became less congested. To Beth's surprise, when the woman sitting next to her got off, Isaac came back and sat next to her again.

"What do you do at the library?" he asked.

A bit shy at his attention, she looked down at her hands and kept her description short. "I run the kids' programme."

"So, you're good with children?" he asked. Most people made that assumption—it was logical.

But Beth smiled lopsidedly. "Oh, not really. The teacher keeps them under control and I talk to them." She wasn't really good with children. If she ever had to manage a class by herself, she panicked. Large groups of children made her nervous. She didn't have much experience with them.

Beth fiddled with her mother's ring. Mum had been much better with children than Beth could ever be. The best she could do was try to remember what it'd been like when she was young and act accordingly. And that didn't always work.

"You enjoy your job?" Isaac asked, interrupting her train of thought.

"Generally, yes." She smiled wistfully. "I love books and a library's the best place for that."

"What are your favourite…" He stopped with an intake of breath and abruptly drew his legs under the seat. "This is where you get off, I believe." He was rising already.

Beth looked around. "Oh yes, it is." She smiled at Isaac, gathering her things together. "I nearly forgot again. Thank you."

Someone else had pulled the cord and the tram was

gliding to a halt.

She stood up and swung around the pole at the top of the steps.

"Thanks!" she called out to the driver, who smiled in the mirror.

As she descended, she waved to Isaac. "Bye!"

"Goodbye, Beth. See you tomorrow." His bright blue eyes sparkled as he smiled.

Bother.

He'd been nice again. Now she didn't know what to think. Was he interested or not? Had she misinterpreted his behaviour? She shook her head as she walked down the alley to the staff door at the side of the library.

Am I ever going to get this right?

FOUR

After a quiet day at work, Beth waited at the bus stop after closing time. She was going through her purse for the right change when she heard a collection of annoyed noises from the people around her.

"Oh, for crying out loud!" said a man nearby.

Beth looked up to find the tram gliding its way down the main street towards them. She smiled to herself and wondered if it would be the same driver.

It was. His rosy face beamed out the front window of the tram. Beth decided to let everyone else get on first, so she wouldn't hold the other passengers up as she chatted to the driver. Perhaps there would be a seat near the front. She was getting used to the new fare and had her purse full of larger denominations now. She held the coins tightly in her hand as she stepped up into the tram.

"Hello, hello!" she greeted him. "What a lovely surprise. Twice in one day."

"Yes indeedy," he replied. "We seem to keep the same hours." He winked at her, which made her grin.

She placed the warm change in the wooden bowl and the

driver scooped it up and gave her a little paper ticket—white with purple writing for the six sections she was travelling.

A seat for one was available behind the front door, across from him, so she perched there.

Clang, clang! went the bell as he took off, the door clacking shut at the same time.

She leant over the aisle and spoke to him. "Am I allowed to talk to you?"

"Absolutely!" he replied.

She held up the ticket he'd just given her. "I used to collect these, when I was a kid."

"Did you now?" His face lit up.

"I had quite a collection at one point. They were about this size and each section had its own colour. Different design to these, of course—different city. Not that they were worth anything."

"Ha! Collections have their own worth, to a child. It's something to do with achievement, I think." The driver paused for a moment, intent on the corner they were rounding, then he spoke again. "You haven't always lived here then?"

"No, I moved here about five years ago, when Mum died. I needed to find better work."

"Ah, sorry about your mum. Your dad passed away, too?" he asked.

"No, he left when I was seven. We haven't seen him since."

"Ah, well, that's no good," he muttered. Beth could see his jaw stiffen as he looked forward. Was he angry for her? How sweet.

"How long have you been driving?" she asked.

A smile popped back onto his face. "Oh, years! I've been driving since I was fourteen. I love it."

"Fourteen's a bit early. What happened there?" she asked.

"I was brought up on a farm. I was taught how to drive a

tractor—one of the first in the area, it was."

"Oh, I see. That makes more sense. I thought you meant you'd been driving buses since you were fourteen."

This made him rock back and forth and laugh outright. "My, my—no. Hold on, there."

They were stopping again and he opened the door. A large number of people boarded, flashing their bus passes at the driver, a few with cash. The driver spoke to every one of them, but received little response. Most didn't even look at him.

Once the door was shut and they were underway, he leaned back and spoke to her again. "I love driving. I can see the world passing by, the city rising around me. The sun shines in on a good day and the suburbs have many a tree to admire as I drive along."

She grinned at him. "You're poetic, too. Do you write?"

"Ho ho—no, I wouldn't presume." He was shaking his head.

They had to stop again a few times as they drove through the city. The driver was friendly to everyone.

"It's a pleasure to see a driver who enjoys what he does," Beth remarked. "So many of them are terse and unfriendly. Sometimes they're even rude."

The driver tutted and shook his head. They trundled through the outskirts of the city and the industrial area.

They crossed the bridge and arrived at the depot area again. As he navigated the complicated network of tracks with the lever on his right, Beth asked, "How do you know which way to go?"

He jerked his head around and stared at her, which perplexed her. The tram slowed down due to his inattention. Perhaps she'd interrupted his concentration.

"Sorry, did I distract you?" she asked, horrified.

"No, no, I'm fine," he said. "I... forgot you were there for a moment." He shook his head, chuckling. "Don't worry, I know this place like the back of my hand. All I need to do is slow down for each switch and keep the lever…" He indicated his right hand. "…either on or off, depending on where I want to go."

He went back to his task and the tram sped up again, heading for a round spot where the network had a particular focus.

"Here," he explained, "I have to do a big turn, so I park on the platform there." He indicated the round spot. "And then I have to turn the tram manually."

He coasted the tram up to and over it, and they came to a halt. He then started down the steps.

"May I come out and see?" Beth asked.

He looked at her and for an instant he froze, his eyes blinking rapidly, but then he shook his head. "No, I'm sorry miss, I can't allow you to do that." She'd never seen him so serious.

She nodded and patted his shoulder. "My name's Beth."

He smiled back and relaxed before stepping down onto the ground.

Beth watched through the window as he walked to a big lever leaning out of the ground at the edge of the spot. Platform—he'd called it a platform.

He clamped the loose handle on the lever closed and moved it to lean the other way. A sturdy board was mounted on a pole and he set his shoulder to it and pushed. Beth was surprised at how easily he spun the entire tram, with its passengers, around on the platform ninety degrees. Beth moved further than she had yesterday, as she was right at the end of the tram, rather than near the middle. And as they turned, the sun appeared from behind the tram's window frame and shone right in her eyes. They must be facing west.

It seemed they were heading the right way now, as the

driver shifted the lever back to its original position and walked back to the door.

He paused again in the middle of the steps and looked Beth in the eye. "Begging your pardon, Beth. I forgot to introduce myself." He held out his hand. "I'm Willis."

Beth shook it, grinning. "Willis, it's a pleasure to meet you."

As Willis resumed his seat, Beth saw movement out of the corner of her eye. A large lady sat on the other side of the aisle—behind Willis—with a wicker basket in her lap. She was smiling at Beth. Beth smiled back, and wondered for a moment whether she was being laughed at. But perhaps not. No matter.

She asked Willis, "How is it so easy for you to turn this whole, heavy thing around by yourself?"

They were off again before he answered. "The wonders of engineering. They keep everything well greased and it pretty much turns itself. I just need to set it going."

"Ah, engineering. Probably mechanical, trams specifically. I could look it up."

"Does engineering interest you, Beth?"

"Interesting things interest me, Willis."

This made him chortle.

"I work in the main library," she explained, and then joked, "The fount of all knowledge and wisdom."

"Sounds like you enjoy it," he remarked.

"Yes, I do. I'm a lucky woman. Lots of people don't like their jobs."

"It's a real shame, isn't it?" Willis said.

Beth continued, "Sometimes I wonder, though, whether people are unhappy because their expectations are too high. I mean, people are *still* starving to death in Africa, religious minorities are being oppressed in the Middle East, and there's more slavery in the world than there's ever been in history before. Perhaps people would be happier if they appreciated what they had, rather than wanting more—or different."

"Slavery? Really?" Willis looked shocked. He shook his head. "But yes, I see what you mean. People should appreciate what they have—that I agree with."

The bell sounded—somebody wanted to get off at the next corner. Willis slowed the tram down, preparing to stop.

"I do go on." Beth excused herself. "You'll find whatever comes into my head will come straight out of my mouth. It's a failing of mine."

Willis glanced at her. "I wouldn't call it a failing. If it's a good mind, the thoughts are worth hearing," he declared.

They came to a halt and the doors opened.

"You're very kind," said Beth, before several people passed between them on their way out.

Three stops later, the tram was all but empty.

"This is me," said Beth. She grabbed her bag from the floor as the tram slowed down again.

She waited until everyone had passed before she stood up.

"Bye, Willis. Thank you."

"See you tomorrow, Beth."

Beth looked up at the tram as it moved away and spotted Isaac in a seat near the back. She lifted her hand as he smiled and waved to her.

She hadn't even seen him when she'd got on. At least she wasn't acting like a lovesick fool today.

Even if she felt like one.

———

Over dinner, Jay grilled her on what had happened with Isaac. Beth told her how, in the afternoon, she'd carefully selected a seat near the front of the tram, so she wouldn't seem like a silly, desperate woman.

But Jay didn't think Beth had acted like a silly, desperate woman.

"You were being your friendly self," she said, "I, for one, *like* your friendly self."

Beth had to smile.

Jay leaned forward over the table. "You are the only person I know who could meet someone on a bus."

"Tram," Beth said.

"Anything. You could meet someone on a lorry full of gypsies, for goodness sake."

"And the driver's lovely, too."

Jay's expression changed. "What kind of 'lovely'? Isn't he older?" She gave Beth a piercing look.

"Yes, yes. I only meant friendly-wise. I'm not interested in the driver. His name's Willis, by the way."

Jay held up her finger then, and smirked. "So, you *are* interested in Isaac, then?"

Beth tutted. "Yes, alright. No point in trying to hide anything from you, is there?"

They ate in silence for a minute or two. Jay had made a delicious beef ragout and Beth had volunteered the bottle of wine from her one and only overseas trip last year. In Tuscany, she'd visited a small, organic winery. They'd served lunch as part of the tour. Sitting on the top of a hill in the sunshine, eating fresh pasta, salami and crusty bread, Beth hadn't been able to resist splashing out on a bottle. She'd been surprised it had made it back in one piece, wrapped in her clothes in the centre of her pack.

She'd had treats like this before and kept them for a 'special occasion', but then ended up either throwing them away or consuming them by herself, which was no fun at all.

So when Beth had discovered that Jay knew a thing or two about good wine—she'd shown Beth her 'cellar'—

they'd decided to celebrate their own special occasion: new flatmates. This was the first time they'd had a chance since Beth had moved in. She'd only just got the last of her stuff put away the night before.

"I like the name Isaac," Jay declared.

Beth shook her head, smiling. She would have to wrestle Jay to get her off the topic.

"Do you know what Isaac means?" Jay asked her.

Beth shrugged—she had her mouth full.

"It means 'he laughs'," said Jay. "From when a woman laughed at God when he told her she was going to have a baby when she was ninety. And then he told her to call him Isaac!" Jay sniggered.

Beth considered for a moment as she took a sip of wine. "I like it. Lots of names are like 'horse-lover', or some sort of flower. 'He laughs' is an action word—a good one."

Jay raised one eyebrow at her. "Let's hope he's an action man—a good one."

They giggled. And not for the last time that evening. The wine was not only *'dee-vine!'*, but half a bottle each was enough to make them both quite jolly.

—— FIVE ——

"Good morning, Beth."

"Good morning, Willis. It's a lovely day today." Beth shook out her umbrella before mounting the steps. Stowing it under her arm, she opened her purse.

"Wet weather can be fun," said Willis. "I need to watch my braking, though—the rain can make me slide farther than usual."

"Of course. It would." Beth placed her fare in the wooden bowl and Willis scooped it up.

As he gave her the ticket, he added, "You know, you can buy a monthly pass now. It's cheaper."

Beth grimaced. "Yes, I know. It's still a lot of money to get together all at once. I'll get there."

Willis nodded but then Beth had to move on as someone else had arrived behind her and wanted to get on.

With no seats available near the front, she looked further down the back. Isaac sat in his usual seat—and he was looking at her. He nodded to the seat next to him.

Well, perhaps he was keen after all. She still hadn't found out if he was married yet. He didn't seem the type to fool around though.

Beth heard the cynic in the back of her mind declare, "All men are the type to fool around." But what was the point in thinking like that?

She sat down and wished Isaac a good morning, then bent and put her umbrella in underneath her heels so it wouldn't roll away. As she did, she noticed a piece of clothing folded under a seat near the back. Strange—it was exactly the same camel colour of Isaac's suit and a matching fedora hat sat on it.

"Good morning," he began. "I hope you don't think I'm being too forward."

Polite as always.

She looked up at him. "Oh, no. I was thinking: at least I gave you a break yesterday from my chattering. Not that I saw you," she added. "I got talking to the driver. He's really interesting." She gave him a sideways grin. "Besides, I don't want to burden you every day, now do I?"

He shook his head. "You're not exactly a burden."

Beth felt herself blush, but before she could respond Isaac went on, "I wanted to ask you: What type of books do you like to read?"

She paused. "I like lots of different kinds, but books about language fascinate me." She leaned back and considered her answer more. "How language changes over time. How different words mean different things to different people." She looked at him. "At different times."

Isaac replied, nodding, "And, of course, language is what books are made of. And you've already told me you love books, which makes you consistent." He leaned towards her and gave her a warm smile, which made her heart flutter.

"Sometimes I wish I knew another language," Beth said. "It gives a person more of an idea about how the brain works behind language." Had that made sense? She tried another way. "I mean, language makes a lot more sense if you understand the culture behind it as well. You could completely get your wires crossed with someone if you don't know the context." She faltered, her eyes sliding to the side. She was blathering on. "Oh, dear," she added. "I'm running out of words."

Though, in truth, she wasn't. She was simply using too many.

"I think I know what you mean," said Isaac.

How generous of him.

*Hmmm! Handsome, witty, intelligent **and** generous!*

Beth tilted her head. "Take, for instance, silence. Now, you don't usually associate silence with language, do you? But it definitely is."

Isaac raised one eyebrow.

"Like music: you need rests and pauses just as much as notes."

He smiled and nodded in understanding.

"There's an Indian tribe." She turned to him suddenly. "Red Indian, you know, not 'Memsahib' Indian. North America." She took a breath. "I can't remember the name of them. But they use silence in a very interesting way. When they meet someone, they can take three days to start talking to them—because they're checking out what quality of person they are first. Then they use silence when a family member comes back after being away. Again, they want to check them out, make sure they're still the same person. And also when someone's angry or grieving."

Isaac was gazing at her, a look of wonder on his face.

Encouraging.

"You see, they think, when someone's angry or grieving, that they're not themselves anymore. Almost like some sort of possession, or loss of sanity. So, they stop talking when someone starts yelling. And they will come and visit someone whose loved one has died, but they'll just sit with them and not speak."

She looked at him. What would he make of that?

His face blossomed into a huge smile. "That is absolutely fascinating!"

Beth grinned at him. "Do you know any foreign languages?"

Isaac was fluent in French and knew some Latin and Italian, too. Thrilled, she asked him to demonstrate his skills and his Italian made her skin tingle.

As per usual, the tram filled and Isaac gave up his seat for a woman left in the aisle. But this time, because they were so intent on their conversation, Beth rose too, and the two of them stood together in the aisle. She couldn't help but notice his smile when she joined him, his blue eyes sparkling at her.

The tram swayed when it changed direction, and they swayed too—sometimes together, sometimes apart as they clung to a leather strap each. Beth felt her breath leave her when Isaac got close and had to stop herself simply gazing up at him. When he had to lean in to speak she felt his breath on her skin. She'd never been so happy to be packed so close to others. It grew quite warm and the windows steamed up.

The pair glided along in their own little world, oblivious to anything else, their voices murmuring in turn. Beth's face pointed up, Isaac's inclined towards her, until the tram stopped and Willis called out.

Isaac prompted her: "Beth. This is your stop, love."

Once again, she hadn't noticed. She bid Isaac goodbye and hurried towards the exit.

"Thanks, Willis!" she sang out as she stepped down onto the road.

And there she was, struggling with her umbrella in a sudden downpour.

Once Beth got the umbrella up, she stood still for a while, her stomach tightening.

It had been an extraordinary ride in. The conversation had been non-stop and so, *so* interesting. There'd been no awkward pauses. Isaac had been truly interested in what she was saying. And he'd practically blushed at one point when they'd got close—she was sure of it. But he hadn't moved away.

"Beth. This is your stop, love."

She gasped.

He'd called her 'love'!

A stupid grin bloomed on her face. Her body pinged with excitement.

Good heavens! How on earth did that happen?

She could barely think straight as she made her way to the library entrance. And her capacity for rational thought did not return to her the entire day.

The clearest point was when she was taking a shift processing the returns. It was an easy job and she was glad of it, having accidentally renamed and misfiled the audiobook database due to inattention. She'd spent over an hour trying to find it again. Her brain hurt.

In the midst of a large pile of returned books, as she swiped them past the code reader, she came across the very one she'd recommended to Isaac the morning before.

Econo-politics: A world transformed from barter to bitcoins.

She stared at it a moment before she logged it back into the system and put it aside.

She would borrow the book herself and show it to Isaac. Using world history since the Industrial Revolution, it exposed the underlying economics without being dry or boring at all. She'd found it a compelling read—and she hoped Isaac would too.

She could barely contain her excitement and the afternoon

went extremely slowly indeed.

Ruby approached her a few minutes before the library closed. "How's the head injury?" she asked.

Beth looked at her, forehead wrinkled, until Ruby smirked. "You've been making so many mistakes today, I thought you must have banged your head," she said, one eyebrow raised.

"Oh, sorry." Beth made a face. "I've been distracted." She could feel herself reddening.

"Is everything okay?" Ruby's look was now one of concern.

Beth smiled back, blushing still. "Yes, everything's okay. I've just had something on my mind. I'm sorry, I'll try and get my act together again for tomorrow."

Ruby let her head fall back. "Alright, Beth. I was a little worried. It's not like you."

Beth smiled. "Well, thank you for caring. Everything's fine."

Ruby nodded. "Great. Have a good evening, then, and I'll see you tomorrow."

"'Night, Ruby."

Beth packed up her things and set off for the stop.

Right on time, the tram pulled up. Beth heard complaints from the other patrons, but she was getting used to that by now. People complained—it was one way to pass the time. Never mind.

The tram was packed and Beth wasn't able to make her way down the back until after they crossed the bridge and a few patrons had disembarked. She stood the whole way and her feet were getting sore, so she was glad to see a pair of women get off at the same time, leaving a two-seater free. And there stood Isaac. They both walked towards the seat: he from the back, she from the front.

Her pulse drummed frantically.

He gestured for her to sit down next to the window. "Good

afternoon, Beth. How was your day?" he asked as he sat down next to her. Their knees touched.

"Oh, pretty good, thank you." She tried to hide her stupid grin as she rummaged about in her bag for the book. "I have something for you to look at."

"Oh?"

Beth had some difficulty getting it out, however.

"What suspense," Isaac added.

She huffed a laugh. "Here we go." Finally managing to extract it, she handed it over.

He held the book for a moment or two, his forehead knotted. He brightened. "Oh, goodness me, this is the book you showed me on your telephone yesterday." His expression of intense surprise—and pleasure—delighted Beth.

He leafed through it. "This looks very interesting indeed."

"I couldn't put it down," Beth said. "The author explores economic and political thought and how they, together, affect how well a society does—especially the lower classes. If you promise not to lose it, I could lend it to you."

He frowned at her. "Would you? Are you sure?"

"Well, it is under my name, so it's me who gets in trouble if it goes missing. Are you likely to lose it?" She couldn't afford to buy a new one, so she certainly hoped he was trustworthy—though she was far from serious.

He chortled. "No, definitely not. I would be so grateful."

"Well, I thought you'd like it." She tried to peel the grin off her face.

"Thank you so much. It's extremely thoughtful of you." He closed the book and set it on his lap. "I should be able to return it in the next couple of days."

"Well, you've got three weeks, so you could take a bit more time," Beth replied.

"Wonderful, thank you again." He paused. "Did you have

any school groups come through today?"

"No, not today. They usually come Monday, Tuesday or Thursday. And we have some weeks go by with none coming in at all—during school holidays. Where did you study?"

Isaac paused for a moment, his brows rising. "Cambridge."

Beth stared at him. "You mean *Cambridge* Cambridge? As in the one in England?" She'd wondered if he was English. He did have the right accent—Northhampton, perhaps.

He nodded and frowned as he looked into his lap.

"Wow! What subjects?"

"Arts and Classics," he replied. He still had his head down, miles away.

Beth couldn't help but smile. "Huh. A classically trained man."

When she replayed what she'd just said in her head, she flushed, though she couldn't have said why.

"I've got a BA in Linguistics," she volunteered.

Isaac's head rose and he smiled. "Linguistics—fascinating. You must tell me about that."

But Beth's stop was coming up. They both rose. It'd been a short meeting this time.

"Well, see you tomorrow, hopefully," said Beth. She held up her finger in a mock-stern sort of way and added, "I will be asking questions about the book."

She was rewarded with a genuine laugh, as Isaac bent his head down towards her. Beth's pulse accelerated. She felt her face redden, so she angled it down and turned away.

"See you tomorrow," Isaac said. He sounded reassuringly certain on the point as he sat down again.

Beth smiled as she stepped onto the pavement, her heart dancing.

It was raining again and, once more, she struggled with her umbrella as the tram moved away.

—— SIX ——

"A classically trained man?" Jay laughed.

"What is it about that phrase I should be embarrassed about?" Beth asked. She wished she'd never said it out loud.

"Nothing. It sounds a little bit old-fashioned, that's all." Jay was sitting at the dining table working on a collage of patterned materials, acrylic and photographs. Beth admired Jay's ability with art and design.

"Old-fashioned? Huh. Isaac all over," said Beth.

"Yeah? What do you mean?" Jay bent over her work.

Beth settled back into the sofa and gave up on the book she'd been trying to read. "I don't know—something about him. For one thing, he doesn't have a mobile."

"What? You're joking."

"No. He doesn't even have access to the internet." Beth shook her head at this, smiling. "He said…" And here she mimicked Isaac. "'I see all these people on here, fiddling with their gadgets.' Like he was an old man or something." Laughing, she thought of other ways Isaac was old-fashioned. "He's extremely polite. He always gets up for women standing in the aisle."

"Oh, nice," said Jay.

"Yeah, I like it. Some woman thought it was sexist or something, but that's nonsense."

"Yeah, I'm with you there."

"You know, we spoke all the way in and…" Beth's heart rate increased. "He does seem to be interested. In me, that is." She frowned and added, "I think."

Jay abandoned her art entirely then, and swivelled around in her chair. "Gosh, really? So, he's not married then?"

Beth's face fell. "Oh, heck, I haven't even looked for a ring." She kept forgetting. Her heart sank.

What if he is married?

That would be awful.

Jay got up and came over to her, sitting down on the sofa. "Well, don't worry too much, but you need to know, don't you? Or you'll get your heart broken." She thought for a moment. "And a ring isn't a definite indicator of him being married, anyway. Maybe you could ask him something like, 'What? Doesn't your wife make you lunch?'"

Beth looked back at Jay, her lips pursed. "You can't be serious."

Jay let out a breath. "Well, perhaps it wasn't the best example, but you know what I mean, don't you? Or, you could ask him, 'Are you married?'" She chuckled, then added with a flip of her hand, "But be casual about it."

Beth shook her head. "No. No, I don't want to do that. That would be so humiliating."

Jay deflated, reconsidering. "Yeah. No, you're right."

Beth had a dreadful night's sleep, swinging from exhilaration about these new encounters, and the possibility of Isaac actually being interested in her, to drowning in the certainty she would find out he was married or discover his complete indifference to her. How could someone so nice not be taken? It wasn't possible.

As a consequence, she was so tired the next morning she nearly missed the tram. In fact she was certain she had, but perhaps her watch was wrong, or the tram came a little late. Either way, she made it—just.

What it did mean was she was last on and in such a rush she was breathless and scrambling to get her purse out. To her relief, Willis told her to pay when she got off instead.

Unfortunately, another woman was already sitting next to Isaac. Her male friend was standing next to her in the aisle, leaning over her, and they were talking intently. She couldn't reach Isaac. Beth contented herself with flicking him a smile and a little wave. He smiled back, inclining his head towards her.

The usual flutter of the heart occurred. This was getting to be a habit.

Not that I'm complaining.

She went almost all the way down the back of the tram and sat next to an elderly woman Beth was sure she recognised.

As soon as she sat down, the lady spoke to her. "Good morning," she said, "I've seen you on here before, haven't I?"

Beth nodded. "Yes, I think I remember you, too."

The woman nudged her arm, smiling. "You gave me your seat the other day, dear. Thank you again." Her head waved about a little as she spoke.

"You're welcome," Beth replied, and then added, "You're brave, catching a rush-hour service. It can get pretty jammed on here." Most retired people waited till the rush was over.

"Yes, indeed it can." The woman nodded. "I'm Matilda. You can call me Tilly, if you like."

Beth grinned at her. "It's a pleasure to meet you, Tilly.

I'm Beth."

Tilly leaned towards her and put her old, arthritic hand on Beth's. It was warm. "And what do you do, dear?"

"I'm a librarian—at the main library. Do you come in there?"

"Oh, no. I'm not much for libraries. I like a nice tearoom. I'd get myself a Devonshire Tea, with lots of jam and cream."

Beth giggled. "Ooo, you're making me hungry, and I've only just had breakfast."

Tilly laughed. "Well, you can't have had enough, then. It's the most important meal of the day, you know." She then added, "Do you know a tearoom that does Devonshire Teas?"

Beth thought. "No, sorry. The only place I've had them at is way out in the country, when I was on holiday. Do you make your own scones?"

Tilly made a face. "No, not any more. I used to make prize…"

Beth suddenly couldn't concentrate on Tilly anymore as, right behind them, in the back seat of the tram, there came a commotion, with a lot of pushing and shoving. Beth turned to see what was happening. Tilly's hand grabbed hers and gave it a strong squeeze.

"I'm just trying to get out," said a schoolgirl in uniform, a large backpack on her back.

"Well, you can ask nicely," said one of the boys who'd pushed Beth aside the other morning. Beth could now see he was blocking the girl's way out.

"I did," insisted the schoolgirl.

"Well I didn't hear you, ya little fat cow. Say it again," sneered the boy.

Inhaling sharply, Beth swivelled her head back the other way and locked eyes with Tilly. They both frowned. The atmosphere in the back of the tram was tense. Beth and Tilly had frozen in place.

The girl's voice was small and pleading. "Please let me out, or I'll miss my stop."

The silence drew out and then the boy finally relented. "Well, I don't want you bawling all over me. Off you go, then, and mind your manners, chubby."

Beth heard a short, sharp sound and the girl gasped as she pushed her way past the boy. She was rubbing her rear end as she made her way to the back door, her head down.

All four of the boys laughed loudly.

"*Ah so!* Chinky Chinaman!" one of them called.

As she descended the steps, the girl turned and her face became visible. Beth could see she was crying, her straight black hair tipping forward over her face.

The atmosphere among the other passengers at the back was now heavy and silent. The easy, dozing quiet had gone, and the air was loud with unlooked glares and swallowed protests.

Why hadn't Beth helped the girl? Was she a coward? And why hadn't anyone else? They were only schoolboys, after all.

Tilly still had a tight grip on her hand.

She must be frightened, poor thing.

Beth rubbed the back of Tilly's hand with her free one.

It wasn't like they could talk about the incident while the bully himself was behind them, so Beth asked Tilly to tell her about her scones.

It wasn't long before Tilly warmed to her subject, though she did occasionally steal a glance over Beth's shoulder.

She also got Beth very interested in scones.

The tram filled. At one point, Beth glimpsed Isaac standing further down the aisle. She was pleased to see he was engrossed in the book she'd lent him.

Not for the first time, she found herself envying how

men could fit everything they needed in their pockets, not worrying about a bag. She always used a satchel, so it could hang from her shoulder and she could use both hands, but what a drag.

Ah, the freedom of carrying nothing!

Isaac had wrapped one arm around a pole and leaned against it, holding the book with both hands, his head bent down towards it. She studied his unselfconscious form.

That camel-coloured jacket did make him look rather handsome. She felt herself colour.

Deep breath. Back to Tilly.

A while later, they'd moved on from scones and Beth was describing the piquant aroma of frying red curry paste, when she sensed someone standing next to her and looked up.

Isaac smiled down at her, the book stowed under his arm. The tram had emptied enough for him to get to her.

Her stomach full of butterflies, she smiled up at him until she remembered Tilly and faced her again.

"Tilly, this is Isaac," she began the introduction and then turned to Isaac's bemused face. "Isaac, this is Tilly—Matilda. She makes marvellous scones, it seems. She's been making me hungry, telling me all about them."

Isaac smiled at Tilly and bent his head in a little bow as he had when he'd met Beth.

Beth found Tilly was now shooing her away, much to her surprise. "You two go and sit together," she said.

Good heavens, is it so obvious?

The back seat was empty. The horrible bullies had gone.

The seat itself was remarkably plush, compared to the rest of the tram's seating. When they'd settled comfortably together, Beth discussed the unpleasant incident with Isaac. He hadn't heard it all and so he listened to her relate the story, his jaw set squarely.

She finished up by saying, "Afterwards, I was so angry at myself for not stepping in and telling him off." She faced Isaac. "Why do I shut down when something like that happens? I'm an adult, for crying out loud. They're just schoolboys."

Isaac was frowning deeply now. "Well, I'm glad you didn't do anything. Those particular boys are a mean bunch. I don't know what they would've done if you'd stepped in. Please stay away from them. They're simply trouble."

Beth argued with him. "That's not right—the bully shouldn't win. But perhaps I could tell the driver what's going on. He could throw them off, couldn't he?"

Isaac looked like he was about to say something, but then reconsidered. Instead, he said, "Yes, good idea—take it to Willis. He's a good man."

Ah, he did know Willis.

Beth took a deep breath.

Well, enough of that.

"How are you finding the book?" Beth asked.

"Oh, wonderful." Isaac leaned back. "Extremely interesting. But…" He paused and his brows descended. "It seems to me that, every time I turn a page there's another war." He took a breath and said quickly, "Though, of course, this isn't a surprise to me. But, still…" His eyes looked far away. "For one so-called reason after another, we turn and strike our neighbour. Over and over." His voice was mournful.

Beth mirrored his expression. "Oh yes, I know. We don't learn, do we? It goes on and on, even now."

Isaac turned to her and looked as if he was going to say something, but then stopped and sighed. "Awful. All those lives. Millions. The twentieth century, for all its advances, was dreadful, wasn't it?"

Beth's heart squeezed tightly, seeing how much the book had affected him.

"We've also had amazing things, though. Penicillin, for example," she suggested hopefully.

Isaac's face brightened. "Yes indeed. Quite extraordinary. And the immunisation against polio and other conditions one thought could never be eliminated. And computing and suchlike."

Beth sniggered. "You do talk like such a toff sometimes." She tried to put on a straight face. "Would that be from your school, do you think, or something you learnt growing up at home? There's quite a debate on which has the stronger influence, linguistically."

With a self-deprecating look, Isaac said, "A bit of both, I would say." He looked at her, his eyebrow raised. "It's a wonder you understand me at all."

Beth grinned cheekily. "Well... most of the time."

Isaac laughed, which set off Beth's heart flutter.

Once again, their time together was cut short by the approach of her stop.

"Well, a pleasure as per usual," said Isaac. "Thank you once more for the book. It's well written, as you promised. I wish you a wonderful day."

"I will do my best," Beth replied, trying hard not to grin stupidly.

She was adjusting how she spoke, she noted, using fewer contractions. What was that called again? That's right— 'speech accommodation'.

In no time I'll be recalling what I did 'as a young lass' and saying 'one really shouldn't'.

She grinned even more.

"I must hear about what you do with *your* day, sometime," she said.

He nodded, stood up with her and walked her to the door. The gesture made her feel extremely special.

But the door didn't open. Beth found Willis' eyes in the mirror.

"Sorry, Beth, I can't let you off until you've paid the fare," he said.

"Oh, of course. I'm so sorry." Beth walked down to him and pulled out her purse.

As she sorted through her change, she saw out of the corner of her eye a man looking at her. He then rotated his upper body around to look at the back door, where Isaac was still standing.

Once she'd put the change in the wooden bowl, she stole a glance at the man. He was scowling at Isaac. Why on earth was he scowling at Isaac?

In return, Isaac's face had set like stone and he stood taller as he watched Beth get off the tram at the front. She waved to him and he nodded back, his face a blank.

Beth's mind raced, looking for some reason for the odd behaviour she'd witnessed. Did the two men know each other? Were they enemies? She couldn't imagine Isaac having enemies. Perhaps they were competitors at work.

It was all she thought about as she made her way down the alley to work. But once she arrived, she had to force herself to focus on the visitors and her guided sessions. Two extra school groups were coming in today, so she was going to be busy.

During her lunch break, a text from Jay arrived:

> **JAY:** I was telling a friend about the tram you catch. He said trams don't run here anymore. Weird!

> **BETH:** Goodness! Then I must have hallucinated my way to work. What did you put in my breakfast?

> **JAY:** LOL!

—— SEVEN ——

Should she ask Isaac about what she'd seen this morning? Surely he would know she'd witnessed the exchange.

But actually, how well did Beth know Isaac? What business was it of hers anyway? They'd only met a few days ago. So far he'd been reticent on details. Not forthcoming at all, in fact. Of course, he had no obligation to tell her all his deep, dark secrets. And did she really want to know?

Really, when it came down to it, he was a complete stranger to her. She didn't even know what he did for a living— management of what?

Actually, she did know something concrete: he'd been to Cambridge. But she still didn't know whether he was married or not. Again, she found herself wondering if she really wanted to know.

Yes, in fact, she did. She must ask Isaac more about himself.

All this was running through Beth's head as she packed up a load of inter-loan books after the last school group left the library mid-afternoon. It was a welcome break from the people she'd had to deal with all day long. The books were to be sent out to the suburban branches.

She was in the small workroom off the corridor between the loans desk and the staff room. This was where they covered and registered new books and repaired the ones that were falling apart. It was full of tape, repair materials and boxes of ready-to-use covers in various sizes.

Several work surfaces and desks filled the room, despite its small size. Beth had spent hours in here, chatting to her workmates while they dealt with large shipments of new purchases arriving all at once. It was so cramped, the previous manager had installed shelves on the wall to store everything until it was needed.

Beth reached up and took the tape—in its awkward dispenser—off the shelf above her. She noticed the shelf was sagging. She must mention it to her boss.

The next thing she knew, Beth was looking up at a blurry face leaning in close. Ruby—yes, it was Ruby.

She was leaning over her. "Beth! Can you hear me?" Ruby had her hand pressed hard against Beth's head, which was throbbing.

The room was spinning, distorting and the lights above her—she was lying on her back—were so bright she had to close her eyes against them.

"Beth! Talk to me. Please!" Ruby's voice was panicked and Beth wondered why.

"What?" she managed to say.

"Beth, you were knocked out. The shelf fell on you."

Beth mustn't talk anymore. If she talked, she would throw up; she knew it. She dragged her hand up to cover her mouth. She didn't want to throw up all over her boss. That would be bad.

She heard Ruby's voice again. "I should put you in the recovery position." She could hear someone else talking in the background.

Ruby moved Beth's body around—her arms and legs—and then she took hold of her shoulder and hip and pulled her onto her side.

Beth threw up.

She felt Ruby pressing the upper side of her head firmly, and her hair being eased away from her face.

"You're gonna be okay, Beth. The ambulance is on its way."

"Guh," was all she could manage.

The ambulance arrived and people bustled around her. They felt her head and neck and talked in reassuring tones. When they sat her up she felt better, but they took her to the hospital anyway. Ruby went with her.

By the time she got to the emergency room, she was wondering what all the fuss had been about. She was feeling so much better, though her head still ached.

The doctor checked her for concussion, flashing a light into each eye and feeling the lump on her head. She asked Beth lots of questions. She had to put a couple of stitches in her scalp as well. Blood covered Beth's clothes.

"Head wounds always bleed badly," the doctor said.

Ruby piped up. "That's what scared the hell out of me—all the blood." She'd stayed in the cubicle with Beth and was sitting in a chair nearby. At least Ruby wasn't someone who fainted when she saw blood. That would've caused an even bigger problem.

The doctor told Beth she must rest and she would have to stay home from work for at least a couple of days.

"But can I go back to work on Monday?" she asked. The weekend was coming up, after all.

"Wait and see how you feel, Beth. But, yes, it's possible." The doctor turned to Ruby. "You'll make sure she doesn't work tomorrow, won't you? Do I have to issue a medical certificate?"

"Oh no. God, no. You won't have any complaints from us,"

Ruby said.

"Good," said the doctor. "Now we have to get her home. Do you have a car?" she asked Ruby, who shook her head but then volunteered to get Beth home in a taxi.

The doctor was satisfied with that and Ruby reassured Beth that work would pay. "It's the least we can do, considering it was our shelf that knocked you out." She then added firmly, "I'm getting all those shelves taken down tomorrow."

The doctor confirmed that Beth had a mild concussion and gave her printed instructions to give to her flatmate. Jay was home on Fridays, so that was going to work well.

By the time they left, it was quite late. Ruby accompanied her in the taxi. They followed a bus for part of the way.

That's when Beth thought of Isaac. And sighed. She wouldn't see him until Monday. Her heart sank.

Will he miss me?

———————

She didn't talk much in the taxi; her head was starting to ache and the bandage was uncomfortable.

Ruby had had the presence of mind to grab both their bags as they were loading Beth into the ambulance. At the front door, Ruby fumbled in Beth's bag for the keys.

Jay got a shock when Beth and Ruby showed up in the kitchen. Beth was ushered into a chair by both boss and flatmate and fussed over with a cool wash cloth and a cup of tea. Apparently, she looked quite awful.

Once Ruby was satisfied that Beth was well cared for, she went home in another taxi.

From then on, Jay became the best nursemaid ever. Beth was soon bundled up in a rug on the couch, having been given a dose of the doctor's painkillers. She soon felt much better, especially once she'd eaten.

All Beth wanted to do then was sleep; she dozed on the couch. Jay woke her up to send her to bed and then woke her once again during the night, as per the doctor's orders.

Late Friday afternoon, Beth remembered what had happened on the tram the morning before. She was on the couch again, with Jay working at the dining table. This time Jay's project was a piece of hardboard, upon which she was painstakingly dotting paint in vivid colours.

"It was busy on the tram yesterday morning," she recalled.

Setting down her brush, Jay gave Beth her full attention, a half-smile on her face. "Oh yes? What happened?"

Beth told her first about the bullies in the back seat and then about the strange man who had glared at Isaac and his response.

"Weird!" said Jay. "Did you ask Isaac about it?"

"I haven't had a chance yet. I won't see him until Monday morning."

"And maybe not even then," said Jay. "You mustn't go to work unless you're feeling a hundred per cent."

Beth looked at Jay coyly. "Yes, Mum."

Jay grinned and wagged her finger at Beth.

———————

Beth slept a lot of Friday and half of Saturday, but time was dragging by the time Sunday afternoon came around.

Beth couldn't wait to see Isaac again. She could remember how he made her feel, but his face wasn't clear in her mind at all. She wished she had a photo of him. She could only remember his keen blue eyes and camel-coloured suit.

Meanwhile, Jay kept an eagle eye on her flatmate all of Sunday, looking for any sign of weakness. But Beth was feeling quite well, so Jay helped her take the bandage off and Beth showered. It was such a relief to wash all the blood out of her hair, though the wound throbbed under the water.

Jay re-bandaged Beth's head and, though it still looked dramatic, it wasn't half as bad as it had been; Beth could cover some of it with her hair.

On Monday morning she left in plenty of time for the tram and stood away from the clump of people at the stop— she didn't want to get jostled. Or moaned at.

Her heart was singing. She tried to quiet it.

I don't even know if he's available. You'll get broken for sure.

She sighed and saw the tram cruising its way down the road towards her. It felt like it was coming just for her. She was grinning like an idiot.

Isaac might not even be on board. Her smile weakened a little.

Willis sat in the driver's chair, as always. The crowd of complaining people, dull to his charms, pushed their way past him and settled like a wave on the shore.

Beth stepped up and put her fare in the wooden bowl.

"Goodness gracious, Beth! Whatever happened to you?" Willis cried as he gave her a ticket and separated the change out into his box. He could do all this without even looking.

"A shelf fell on my head last Thursday and knocked me out. I had to take Friday off work." She tried to make it sound trivial.

"Oh, my dear! We were wondering where you were. You must take better care of yourself."

Beth smiled and moved down the aisle.

We?

Isaac was standing already, right next to the back door, his features strained. The seat on the aisle was vacant and he waved her into it.

He asked the same question Willis had. Beth related the story and the crease in Isaac's forehead deepened. He stood next to her for the entire journey—to protect her from the pressing crowd. He crouched when he could, looking up into her face, examining it.

He returned the history book, expressed his gratitude and eagerly began to discuss the 1929 and 1987 financial crashes, before breaking off when he saw her rubbing her forehead.

"You look pale. Are you quite alright? Are you sure you should be going to work?" he asked. He placed his hand on hers, on her knee.

She'd been wondering the same thing, in fact, but couldn't possibly regret being the subject of his special attention this morning.

But is this the only way I can get you to stay with me all the way in?

"I will take it slowly," she promised, her voice subdued. "But I was getting bored at home."

"Well, I shan't tax you too much before your workday," he said cautiously. "We can discuss it at a later time. It is an excellent book."

Beth smiled wanly. "I look forward to it."

On her part, Beth studied his face as they talked about lighter things. What colour was his hair? What shape his jaw, his cheekbones? How full were his lips? Would she remember now?

When they came to the depot and Willis stepped off to turn the tram, Beth spied the older man she'd seen last week. Sitting up the front again, he was watching her with Isaac through the motionless bodies of their fellow-passengers, his expression worried—for what reason, she couldn't guess. He was tall and thin, his face hawk-like. She guessed he was in his fifties.

After they'd crossed the bridge, people started getting off and Isaac crouched so Beth could look him in the face again.

What a handsome face.

"What do you do, Isaac?" Beth asked softly.

He blinked and looked down. "I manage a company of people regarding the maintenance of property," he said.

He stopped.

"Property management?" Beth looked at him, frowning. She didn't understand. It didn't seem right.

"Yes. Gardeners, cooks, cleaners—many older people among them. Lots of valuable experience, in my opinion."

The tram stopped again and Isaac had to stand to let people pass him in the aisle. Beth heard several sets of heavy footsteps approaching from the back and Isaac moved even closer to her, placing his left hand on top of the seat back behind her head, his hip against her shoulder.

It was the bullies. One of them shot her a dirty look as he thumped down the steps to the pavement below.

Once they'd gone, she looked up at Isaac's face. His eyes had followed them off the tram and he was biting his lip.

Was he afraid of them?

He caught her looking at him, smiled and bobbed down onto his haunches again, grasping the armrest of her seat and the pole opposite.

She looked at his left hand. No ring.

Beth felt a sudden lightness of heart.

Now, hold on a minute. That doesn't mean he's not married.

Warmth radiated through her body.

Too late.

"Tell me about your flatmate," he asked. The word sounded awkward on his tongue.

She'd mentioned before how wonderful Jay had been during her recovery.

"She's a lovely woman. Quite artistic," said Beth. "She works at an art gallery near the beaches. She does photography, painting and montages on canvas—mixtures of paint and materials. Oh, here's one."

Beth whipped out her phone and opened the photos. She'd taken a photo of one of Jay's artworks on the wall in the front room.

Isaac stared at the image on the phone for a moment. "It's a camera as well?" He was slowly shaking his head.

Beth giggled at him—her joy was ridiculous—and said, "Lordy, yes. You should really get a phone, you know. Here…"

Feeling reckless, she tilted her phone at him and tapped the circle on the screen. *Click!*

She brought the photo up and showed him. His response was extraordinary: he stared at the photo on the screen as if he hadn't seen himself for years.

Her laugh seemed to bring him to himself. "Well, well! I didn't realise you'd done that," he said.

She shook her head gently. "I should really ask permission beforehand."

But she was only half serious.

I've got a photo!

She couldn't wait to show Jay.

They arrived at Beth's stop—far too soon—and Isaac stepped back to give her room to get off. He held out his hand to help her up.

She smiled at him. "See you this evening—I hope."

He smiled back, his eyes warm. "I'll be here." His expression became serious. "Don't work too hard. Look after yourself," he cautioned her.

"I'll be fine."

But the first step down gave Beth's head quite a jolt and she had to grip the handrails to make sure she didn't do it again. Willis waited patiently.

Once she was off, she gave Isaac a little wave as the door closed and the tram set off again. He'd remained standing at the top of the stairs, a slight frown on his face.

It still doesn't mean he's not married.

I don't care.

Oh, yes you do.

— EIGHT —

Ruby had her on light duties for the day, and Beth was glad of it—she was still getting tired easily. However, she did make it through most of the day.

She spent her time in the little workroom again, but Ruby had fulfilled her vow to have the shelves removed and the room felt larger for it. They still had to figure out where to put all the boxes of covers, which were piled in one of the corners.

The morning was full of administrative work: making lists of when inter-loans were due back and checking on back orders. Light work, really, but the room was stuffy, so she was glad to get out of it at lunchtime.

But she was back to it again afterwards: a pile of book repairs and scratched CDs to resurface. Beth did her utmost for the rest of the day, though she felt waves of tiredness coming on by mid-afternoon. Near the end of the day, Ruby just happened to walk into the workroom when Beth was struggling to keep her eyes open, her head nodding.

"Right, off you go, Beth. You've done well, but we'll make it a short day." Ruby shooed her out of the building.

Beth was tired and she did need to go home, but it would mean catching an earlier service and she wanted to see Isaac again today.

There was no arguing with Ruby, though, and Beth got her things together and trudged towards the exit. She went as slowly as she could, but was still well before her usual time. She sat at the stop, head lowered.

So she couldn't believe her eyes when she saw the tram—her tram—trundling towards her soon after she'd arrived at the stop. She rubbed her eyes—she actually, physically rubbed her eyes: she must be dreaming. But no, she heard the familiar electric zing and the doors clacked open right in front of her.

She clambered aboard and stared at Willis. "You're early!" she cried. She was, for a change, the only one getting on at this stop.

"I know," he said. "It's the queerest thing. I had to switch a shift with another driver. And here you are." He beamed and nodded. "It was meant to be."

Shaking her head a little, and then regretting it—her headache was coming back—she placed her change in the familiar wooden bowl. Willis swiped it up and handed her the ticket.

"You look tired, Beth, love. Best sit down straight away, eh?" he said.

She nodded, found the nearest empty seat and settled herself in. She wouldn't be up for much chatting this evening. She closed her eyes.

"Are you alright, dear?" asked the woman next to her. She was a generously proportioned woman with a broad, kindly face and red hair gathered up in a bun. She had what Beth guessed to be a Scottish accent.

"I'm quite tired, actually," Beth admitted, her voice weak.

"You look like you've been in the wars. Are you hungry at all?" the woman asked. Her voice was soft and sweetly lilting.

Come to think of it, Beth was hungry. It'd been a long time since lunch. Perhaps that was why she was so tired.

"Yes, I am," said Beth.

"Well, look here. I've just made these. Would you like one?" She lifted a cloth in the basket she held in her lap. Underneath were pastries and small rolls.

Beth hesitated.

Willis had overheard and he spoke out at this. "Oh, you lucky thing. Fresh baking from Margie. I recommend it, Beth. It'll make you feel better." He was very enthusiastic.

Being so worn out, Beth was overcome with the warmth she was being shown and she ducked her head and swallowed hard. She reached out and took a cheesy-looking roll. She liked cheese.

"Thank you so much," she mumbled.

The roll was still warm, and when Beth tore it in half, the smell filling her nostrils was divine. She relished every mouthful and felt better for the nourishment, as well as the care.

"That was lovely. Thank you again," she said to her neighbour.

"One more, eh? Take a sweet one, for dessert," Margie replied. Again, she lifted the cloth.

Beth chose a simple sweet pastry and that disappeared almost as quickly as the roll had. It, too, was fresh and warm.

After this, energy filled her. She could lift her head now and she looked properly at her seat mate.

"So, you're a baker are you Margie?" she asked.

Margie nodded and smiled. She appeared suddenly shy.

"Well, you're a good one," said Beth. "You've lifted my spirits. Thank you so much."

Margie smiled again and bent her head, hiding, despite the size of her. Beth found her behaviour rather sweet and wanted to draw her out and get her talking. Kind people were always worth knowing.

"Where did you learn to bake?" she asked.

Margie's eyes were large now, her head on a coy lean. "I learnt most of it from me mother."

"She was a good baker, then," Beth said.

"Ay, she were way better'n me." By the look in Margie's eyes, she had fond memories of her mother.

"My mum wasn't much of a baker, but she could cook a great casserole. I've got lots of her recipes and I keep trying them, but they never taste the same," Beth admitted.

"Ay, there's something extra you can never write doon." Margie nodded.

"So, you work as a baker in town?" Beth asked.

Margie paused. "I do a wee bit of cookin', yes."

"More than baking?"

"Used to be."

"Are you the only one who's inherited your mum's cooking ability? Any siblings?"

Margie's face dropped a little. "Not anymore."

"Oh, I'm sorry. I'm a bit nosey, aren't I?" said Beth.

"Not at all." Margie's smile returned a little. "What happened te yer head?"

Beth related the story and Margie visibly relaxed as Beth took over the work of talking. Margie was a good listener, bless her.

Beth continued to coax Margie to talk as well, and she found out, bit by bit, where Margie was from and tidbits of her life and work.

"Speaking of baking," Beth said, though they'd not been talking about baking for some time now, "there's another woman I met on the tram who told me all about the prizewinning scones she used to make."

On the off chance Tilly might be aboard, Beth turned to look behind her. The tram was half full by then from having passed through the industrial area. They stopped work a little earlier than the city workers.

Tilly sat about halfway down the tram, staring out the window. Beth pointed her out to Margie.

"Oh, yes, Tilly made lovely scones, she did," replied Margie.

Beth's eyes widened. "Goodness, you know her already?"

"Oh, ay. She's been catching this tram for years now. We've had a good old natter in the past." Margie's face was bright with familiarity.

Beth giggled. "Heavens above. I'm a relative newcomer, then. How long have you been catching the tram?"

Margie's face became guarded. "Oh, I don't know. Long time." She looked away, her expression sombre.

That was strange.

Unfortunately, turning to look for Tilly had been a bad move. It'd made Beth's headache worse and she had to sit facing forward with her eyes closed for a while, taking deep breaths to try to relax her neck muscles.

Margie left her alone, and Beth sat in silence until Willis said gently, "Here you are, Beth, love."

She opened her eyes. "Oh, thank heavens for you, Willis. I'd have been all over the city by now if you weren't looking out for me."

He beamed at her, but his smile faded as he watched her stand up carefully.

"Do you need a hand, Beth?" he asked.

"Thanks, Willis, but I'm up now and I'll keep hold of the rails as I go down. Sorry for the delay."

"Oh, never mind that. You take your time," he said.

Dear Willis sat on the edge of his seat and watched her like a hawk as she descended the steps to the pavement. Beth was sure he would have jumped up and grabbed her if she'd shown any hint of falling.

Once she'd landed, she lifted her hand in a wave. "Thanks, Willis. See you tomorrow, hopefully." Her voice was sounding weak, so she hoped he could hear her.

His smile returned in full force. "Ta-ra, then. Take care." He closed the door and the tram moved off.

Beth watched it pass her and then had to look again. Was that Isaac in the back of the tram? But the second look left her with some doubt. Had that been his camel-coloured jacket or not?

It couldn't possibly be him. Isaac wouldn't be travelling home this early. No, of course it couldn't have been him.

Surely the day had had enough coincidences in it.

— NINE —

Beth got better every day and each morning Isaac would sit with or stand next to her for the entire journey. He wouldn't let her stand.

She loved every minute.

In the afternoons—she made it to closing time for the remainder of the week—the tram was often packed before she got on and she sat with Willis or Margie up the front, and occasionally with Tilly, if she could get a little further down the tram. Once enough people got off, Isaac would come up from the back and join her.

She wondered why he didn't sit up the front. She hoped it wasn't because of the older man who was always so stern and gave Isaac cold looks when he came up the front. When she got off, she often saw Isaac walking down the back again. What was it between the two men?

But then, if it wasn't that issue keeping him up the back, it would mean Isaac wasn't as interested in her as she would have hoped. So neither option was preferable.

A nurse removed the stitches on Wednesday night. Beth was bemused to receive hearty congratulations during her morning commute.

Jay agreed with Beth: Isaac was handsome. Jay had studied the image for quite some time.

"He looks really…" Jay paused. "Well… intelligent, actually. And, yes, I see what you mean about him being old-fashioned. The shirt he's wearing—that collar's supposed to go with a cravat. But who wears those these days?"

Beth wished Jay could meet him.

"Why don't you come to work with me one morning? Then you could check him out for me," she suggested.

Jay's eyes brightened. "Yeah, okay. But it won't be for a while—I'm busy at the moment."

Beth resolved to keep asking her until the right time came.

"But, surely," Jay said suddenly, "it'd be better if you asked him back here for dinner or something, wouldn't it? Why don't you?"

The idea gave Beth a spark of excitement and then a pang of nerves. It also brought up something that'd bugged her the night before.

"You know, he hasn't ever asked me for my phone number or anything," she said. "I mean… doesn't that mean he's not really interested?"

Jay was quiet for a while before she said, "Well, in the worst case it might. Best not to assume the worst straight away, though. It's only been a few weeks. Perhaps he's nervous, too. Maybe he needs more time. And…" She stopped, a pensive look on her face. "Well, you've never actually found out if he's available, have you?" She looked sidelong at Beth who frowned and looked away. As Jay had mentioned before, just because Isaac didn't wear a wedding ring didn't mean he wasn't married.

This cold, hard fact came to mind more often than she would like to admit. Mostly when she wasn't with Isaac. But she was still too uncomfortable about asking him straight out. She would simply have to wait and see if he would make a move of some sort.

She gave Jay a weak smile. "You keep your fingers crossed."

The next morning—Friday—Beth watched Isaac as closely as she could and tried to determine what signs she could take as certain. But—she had to be frank—nothing he did pointed one way or the other. Perhaps he was merely being friendly after all.

Good grief!

His interest in Beth was still as much in question as it had been at the beginning. Surely she couldn't be so wrong about the signals.

After another long conversation with Isaac on the way into the city, she decided she just had to relax and assume he would get around to it when he could. She would just enjoy his company in the meantime and hope for the best.

More than the usual throng of people were at the stop the next Thursday evening and Beth was lucky to get aboard at all. She managed to squeeze herself on before Willis told the ones behind her to catch the next service. Many loud complaints were heard, but there was plainly no room. The last few passengers pulled their rear ends or bags inside the tram and Willis managed to shut the door.

"Pay later, will you Beth?" he asked over the heads of those between them.

Beth was stuck in the stairwell, so that suited her just fine. "Of course." She grinned at him.

It meant they didn't stop at all until they'd crossed the bridge and people began to get off. In the meantime, the crush of people was hot and the smell of too many bodies pressed in on her.

Beth found a seat not long after, next to a thin woman with a pinched face wearing a beautiful dress. The ruffled skirt was a dark mauve and was long enough to cover her ankles. The bodice was tight, which was supposed to accentuate the figure she was sadly lacking. Her half-clad, bony arms held an umbrella, the point resting on the floor. She wore a hat with a curled brim and decorated with colourful feathers.

"What a beautiful hat," said Beth. "Where did you find it?"

The woman's eyes widened, as if she were shocked Beth would dare speak to her.

"Well, thank you very much," she said. "I found it in London, actually." Her accent was plummy.

Beth was envious. "Oh, you've been to London? I'm so jealous. I'd love to go there. Did you enjoy it? How long did you stay?"

The woman's face assumed a gracious smile. "Well, yes, I did enjoy visiting London. We went every year when I was growing up."

Beth grinned. "Ah, I thought I heard an English accent. When did you come here?"

The stiff smile diminished a little. "Well, you know, I don't actually remember." She paused, looking down. "We have been here quite some time, though." She nodded to herself.

"Well, it's lovely to meet you. I'm Beth."

The woman blinked twice, took and held her breath for a moment and then nodded again. "A pleasure to meet you. I'm L…" She stopped completely as her eyes bulged a little before she finished: "Maxine."

"Maxine. A pleasure," Beth responded.

After another moment's pause, Maxine spoke again.

"May I assume you catch the tram frequently?" she asked.

Bemused at the formality of the question, Beth answered simply: "Yes."

Maxine drew in a long breath. "Then I wonder if you might know my fiancé, Isaac Lyttelton?" She fixed a cold, unsmiling gaze upon Beth. Her expression had changed suddenly—she knew the answer already.

The shock left Beth painfully hollow and she felt the blood drain from her face.

Oh, what a fool I am!

All she could do was nod as her dry mouth formed her inane reply: "Uh huh."

Why didn't he tell me about his fiancée?

Maxine raised a single eyebrow, never once looking away. "He's such a pleasant man, isn't he? So generous and affable."

Beth had to face the front as she couldn't bear to look at Maxine any longer. "Absolutely. He's charming." She attempted her former cheerfulness.

"He's mentioned you, Beth," Maxine stated. "He finds you entertaining, and quite willing to please."

Entertaining?

Beth was mortified at Maxine's wording.

"You lent him a history book, I believe?" said Maxine.

"Yes." Beth stared at her hands. "I work at a library."

"A library," Maxine said with a laugh. "How quaint. You enjoy that, do you?" Maxine's tone conveyed an arrogance Beth had seldom encountered. She felt abruptly insignificant in the presence of someone wondering at her sanity. How could she possibly enjoy such an activity?

Hold on a minute!

Maxine had gone too far. After an instant of feeling irrelevant and trivial, reason kicked in and Beth's anger rose within her.

Who do you think you are?

"Yes, I do," Beth replied, finally raising her head and fiercely returning Maxine's gaze. "I'm honoured to work in such a stimulating environment." She went on the offensive. "And you? Do you do anything? Other than sit on trams insulting people?"

The corner of Maxine's mouth rose a little. "My aren't we prickly? Have I touched a nerve, perhaps?"

Beth met her eye to eye. "Yes, you have and I don't see why I should pretend you haven't. I like to contribute to society and I appreciate others who do the same. Those who don't grasp the value of work—" She swept her eyes down Maxine's emaciated form. "—and sit around mocking people who actually do something mean very little to me, especially if they think they're better than I am."

Maxine feigned shock. "Whatever gave you that idea?"

Beth's smile was stiff. "Your choice of words, your use of tone and your body language. Have you read anything about body language, Maxine?"

The blank look now in Maxine's eyes told Beth she hadn't, so, feeling emboldened, Beth went on to explain: "Communication is far more than words, and if you think you can pretend otherwise, you need an education beyond primary school." She handed Maxine her business card, which she'd slipped out of her purse. "Come and visit me at the library and I'll show you a book or two that'll help you understand this simple concept."

Maxine didn't offer an answer and she wordlessly took the card.

Beth faced the front of the tram again and saw Willis, grinning fit to burst, though he was facing forwards too, supposedly concentrating on his driving. Perhaps he'd heard.

Beth looked around and noticed a seat was now available next to Tilly, who was a row behind, on the other side.

Thank goodness!

Beth excused herself to Maxine and slipped out of the seat to join Tilly.

"Hello Beth, dear. Lovely to see you," said Tilly, whose body language said exactly the same thing.

Beth inhaled to steady herself. "Hello Tilly. Great to see you, too." Though she was still smarting from Isaac's dishonesty.

Tilly leaned closer and spoke in an undertone. "Don't worry, dear. Maxine's nasty to everyone."

Beth had to cover her mouth to stop from laughing too loud and then frowned as she realised what that meant. She looked back at Tilly. "You know her?"

"Oh, yes." Tilly rolled her eyes. "She seems to think she's engaged to Isaac. She's nothing of the sort. Funny old thing." Her voice was still at low volume.

Beth suddenly felt light as a feather. Isaac hadn't been deceiving her, then. What an awful few minutes she'd had. She was so distracted by it she forgot she hadn't paid and found the door refusing to open.

"Sorry, Beth. Can't let you off until you've paid your fare." Willis grinned at her in the mirror.

———

"And that surely means he's not married," said Jay. They'd set out on a walk after dinner.

Beth nodded and the two of them grinned at each other.

"That's what I was hoping you'd say," said Beth. "'Cause I thought the same thing and then wondered whether I was fooling myself." Her brain was short-circuiting again and she'd wondered at her own sanity. Was this 'being in love'?

"Well, there is the slightest chance we're wrong." Jay shook her head. "But I think it's highly unlikely."

They walked along together for a while in companionable silence before Jay slowed.

"That means Tilly knows Isaac, too," she said. "And doesn't that mean *all* the people you know on the tram know each other?" Her face crinkled up. "Isn't that a little weird? How long have these people been travelling together?"

"Oh, yeah," said Beth. "Looks like they've been catching the same service for a few years and they've got to know each other. It's not that startling. They're all friendly people." Her smile drooped a little. "Except for Maxine."

"Huh! What a cow!" Jay didn't say much more as she was puffing from the hill they were climbing.

Beth was so grateful for Jay's support. And her validation of Beth's fragile hope for more with Isaac.

— TEN —

Beth wasn't enjoying weekends as much as she used to. For her it meant two whole days during which she wouldn't see Isaac.

She often felt a little giddy when she thought about Isaac and the conversations they'd enjoyed together. She had great difficulty maintaining her concentration at work. She'd had no idea how useless she would become under such circumstances.

But she couldn't complain. She set Isaac's photo as her phone's wallpaper. Later she realised he might see, and she felt more than a little creepy, so she changed it back.

Madness.

She woke bright and early the next Monday morning— post Maxine—and arrived at the stop in good time. The journey was full of a lively debate with Isaac about whether society changed language or language changed society, and then the busyness of work distracted her—a little—during the long wait for the journey home.

In the evening, Beth was again stuck standing down the front of the tram. Tilly was sitting close by and they smiled and nodded to each other. Beth was looking forward to chatting with Tilly.

Just before the tram crossed the bridge, the four bullyboys pushed their way on. Beth couldn't believe how rude they were and what they assumed they could get away with.

The tram was entering the depot area and the boys obviously wanted to get down the back as they started shoving people out of the way. Nobody objected—except for Beth.

"Excuse me, but it's not right for you to treat people like that," she said. Her heart was racing.

One of the boys responded, "Shut up." He stuck his face right up to hers.

Beth stood her ground and glared at him. Willis was outside, turning the tram around.

"Don't look at me like that," the boy said and then spied Tilly frowning at him too. "And you neither." And then he used the most abusive and foul term Beth had ever heard— at Tilly! It was one thing to call the schoolgirl a fat cow to her face—so hurtful and debasing—but this was beyond imaginable, and utterly unrepeatable.

Beth's anger rose up even more. "How *dare* you speak to an elderly lady like that?" Her voice was at its loudest. "That is not acceptable. Get off!"

Willis had re-boarded by now and he froze at the top of the steps, staring at Beth, wide-eyed. No one else was looking at all.

"Get stuffed!" said the boy.

"I will not. You're getting off!" Beth reached over and grabbed him by the ear.

"Ow!" he yelled, "Gerroff!"

But no way was she letting go. She dragged him towards the open door.

"You can jolly well walk," she exclaimed. She wouldn't use

any bad language; she was not about to be accused of hypocrisy.

The few people forward of her didn't even bother to move aside as she marched him to the front and then down the steps. Once he was on the lowest step, she gave him a deft shove in the back, sending him down onto the depot floor.

The boy stood staring at Beth, his eyes like globes as she heard a bone-chilling shriek in the distance which made her insides tense up.

A fox? At this time of day?

She must be imagining things. They didn't have foxes here.

But the boy jumped and his face paled. He looked so scared, she almost relented. But it was the middle of the day; he would be fine. She shrugged it off.

"Close the door, please, Willis," she said. Willis would have heard the sound. She would ask him later.

Willis was back at his post now and complied. His face was taut as he drove the tram away.

"Sorry," said Beth in a quieter tone. "I would've got you to do it, but you were outside." She explained further. "He said something despicable to Tilly. He had to be taught a lesson."

He looked at her and nodded, smiling. "You're a good woman, Beth."

She scoffed at him and moved back to where she'd been before. The other three boys had retreated to the rear. Then, quite suddenly, the tram came to life as conversations resumed.

Tilly smiled at Beth, though her eyes didn't join in entirely. "Thank you, dear. You're a lovely girl."

A little while later, the woman sitting next to Tilly got off and Beth took her spot.

She grinned at Tilly, determined to leave the unpleasant episode behind. "I tried your scone recipe on the weekend. It went really well," she said.

"Oh, did you, dear? How wonderful. I haven't been able to bake for an age," said Tilly. She gave Beth a wide smile.

"Well, you know, I could bring you some. Where do you live?" It couldn't be far away from where Beth lived and she and Jay could drop by on their walk.

Tilly blinked at her for a second or two. "Oh, I live at the end of the line, Beth, dear. It's a lovely old area." She went on, "But why don't you pop some in your bag for tomorrow morning? You don't have to make a special journey for me." She leaned towards Beth and lowered her voice confidentially. "I can't take visitors, dear." She patted Beth on the hand as her head bobbed about.

Beth nodded in understanding, though she wasn't sure she did. "Oh sure. Never mind. I'll bring some in tomorrow morning."

After a few more stops drained the tram of more of its passengers, Beth found Isaac standing next to her. With no available seats nearby he crouched down next to her.

So close.

"You're a brave woman," he said, quite seriously.

She laughed. "Well, we have to look after each other, don't we? Especially friends." She glanced over at Tilly, who beamed back. She felt like she'd joined an exclusive club of exceptional people. "Perhaps I should bring you all some scones tomorrow morning. Though they're not as good without jam and cream, are they?"

A winning smile spread over Isaac's face. Beth's heart squeezed.

She sighed and asked him, "Do you live at the end of the line as well?"

With a quick glance at Tilly, he smiled. "Yes."

"I must come and see where all the nice people come from."

To Beth's dismay, the smile fell from Isaac's face and

he said, "Oh, no. There's not much to see." He cleared his throat, and added, somewhat formally, "I look forward to your scones in the morning."

Isaac then stood up and walked away. The conversation was over.

Perhaps his legs were getting sore. Or perhaps she'd pushed too hard—been too nosey again.

It's nearly time to get off anyway.

She kept trying to reassure herself, but Beth couldn't shake the horrible feeling she'd said something wrong. But what? The atmosphere had changed just a hint—but that hint had driven him away.

———

"But why is it so wrong to want to visit friends at home?" asked Jay later.

"I don't know. I'm sure…" Beth stopped and re-started. "I think I…" But she was lost. She was attempting to be positive, but finding it difficult to keep fighting the growing evidence pointing to the negative.

"I'm confused, actually," she admitted. Beth could feel her face sagging. She'd been so hopeful. She'd been so sure Isaac was interested in her. She'd been wrong. How had she been so mistaken about the signals?

Finally, she let out a long sigh and said, "I don't know what to think."

"No. I can see that," Jay replied. After a short pause, she went on, "I think you should ask him." She nodded. "Straight out."

Beth stared at Jay as she kept talking.

"With all you've told me, I don't think you've been silly in your assumptions. If he's not interested in you, then he's deceived you, whether he's meant to or not. It's not right."

Beth's insides squeezed painfully. "What? Ask him flat out?"

Jay raised one eyebrow. "Yes. Why leave him in control?" Jay placed her hand on Beth's shoulder. "He's taken you on an emotional roller coaster and you owe it to yourself to stop it. You have nothing to lose. If he's interested, good; you can take it further. If he's not, then you can move on and not waste any more time wondering."

But what about all the emotions she had invested in this?

"I'm not sure I have nothing to lose," she murmured.

Jay was chewing the inside of her cheek now. "Well, I'm not saying it won't hurt if he says he's not interested. What I mean is: you haven't given or promised him anything other than excellent conversation. You've only ever seen him on the tram. If you want to make sure you don't lose any more of your heart, you need to find out what he wants." She paused for an instant and looked away. "And what he doesn't."

Beth spent the rest of the evening cleaning the bathroom until it gleamed. As if she could scrub away her anxieties. But she forgot to wear gloves, so the chemicals wrecked her hands, and she still didn't sleep well.

Late the next morning, she ran to the stop and arrived just as the tram was about to pull out.

"Come on Beth, hop on," said Willis, beaming down at her.

Beth was breathing hard. "Thanks, Willis, you're a champion."

"You'll get fit doing that every day," he countered as he took her fare and gave her the ticket.

She grinned at him.

Isaac sat in his usual seat. Beth was tempted to sit somewhere else to avoid the confrontation, but it wouldn't help, would it? Besides, where else could she sit?

She walked towards him, pausing where Margie and Tilly were sitting together, halfway down the aisle, and giving them the scones she'd promised. Her heart was squeezing painfully in her chest. She braced herself.

I don't really want to do this. But Jay's right, I can't go on fooling myself. Or letting him fool me.

Isaac was smiling at her as she sat down, which wilted her resolve a little.

He spoke even before she'd settled. Not wanting to waste time, it seemed, Isaac launched straight into his favourite subject of conversation—history—as she passed him a scone. He acknowledged this with another bright smile.

"Good morning," he said. "You mentioned that one of the causes of the Second World War was the swing to fascism in both Italy and Germany. That fear of communism continued afterwards, though, didn't it?"

Isaac seemed so sophisticated and knowledgable in so many areas. He knew all the artists in the Impressionist movement and the progression of the French Revolution. He'd travelled to Italy, too. And yet sometimes the questions he asked made it sound like he was hearing it all for the first time.

The conversation on communism distracted Beth for a while, as they moved from the 1917 Revolution to the Cold War—she promised to lend him her copy of The Crucible— and then, in no time at all, Isaac was excusing himself and standing up for a woman in the aisle. The transaction happened so abruptly Beth never got a chance to join Isaac in the aisle before she was pinned next to the window by the woman. Isaac made his way down the back.

This habit was beginning to frustrate Beth, as he could just as well stand in the aisle and talk to her from there. She suspected he thought it rude to talk over someone. Usually, Beth would agree, dammit.

But they often had a chance to sit together again later on, once the load of passengers decreased in number. She would bring it up then.

Beth was in the middle of moisturising her dry, chapped

hands when this happened—after they'd crossed the bridge. Once again, it happened suddenly. She'd just squeezed some cream out onto her palm.

Not wanting to be distracted from her purpose this time, Beth forced herself to speak as soon as Isaac sat down.

"Isaac?" She tried to ignore her thudding heart as she stowed the tube of moisturiser back in her bag.

"Yes, Beth," Isaac said as he looked at her with his clear, blue eyes.

The breath left her body, but she swallowed and forged ahead.

"I do enjoy our conversations," she said. "You're so easy to talk to. Most people aren't interested in chatting."

"Intelligent conversation is a satisfying activity. I, too, enjoy our interaction," he replied. Why did he have to put it so formally?

Ah well, good sign anyway.

"Perhaps we could extend our conversations by meeting at other times, in more leisurely surroundings," Beth suggested, her head tilted, eyebrows raised.

Isaac paused for a long time and Beth watched the smile drain away from his face. Her heart sank... right to the bottom of her stomach.

"I would li..." He stopped and, looking away, began again, slower this time. "That won't be possible Beth." Isaac then sat still, looking down at his hands in his lap.

Did he nearly say he would like to?

"Are you married, Isaac?" asked Beth. She needed to clarify *something*. She needed some reason why.

He looked up as he spoke. "No." Then he stopped and stared at her, like a deer caught in headlights. He looked for a while as if he would say something more, but nothing came out. Shutting his mouth, he returned to staring at his hands.

"Isaac, I'm confused," said Beth. "The way you've been

behaving made me think you were interested in me… in a relationship. But you say now you don't want to see me anywhere but here, on this tram. I don't understand. Have I got the signals wrong?"

Another long pause and then his head rose and he gasped, as if in discovery. "Yes. Yes, I'm afraid you've read the signals all wrong, Beth. I'm not interested in pursuing a romantic relationship with you. I was merely being friendly." His smile was stiff and awkward, his tone as standoffish as Maxine's had been.

Beth was stunned. She sat in silence, feeling as if her insides were withering.

How humiliating!

She didn't know what to say.

"This is your stop, Beth," Isaac said, a little too robotically, as he rose and stood in the aisle. He was looking at her only out of the corner of his eye.

"Oh." Her body felt like lead as Beth dragged herself out of her seat and down the steps.

"Bye, Beth!" called Willis.

She couldn't respond. Something was stuck in her throat.

Once her feet hit the ground, she looked up the stairs and took a last look at Isaac. It still didn't make sense. Why did she feel like he was lying to her?

Before the door shut between them she caught a glimpse of his expression. His eyes were lowered, his lips pressed together and he was rubbing the back of his neck. This confused her even more; he looked upset.

Beth's eyes followed the tram as it moved away. Instead of sitting down, she saw Isaac walk to the front of the car and, though she couldn't see clearly, it looked like he sat down— next to the older man she'd seen glaring at him before.

Beth remained where she'd landed, numb, until a bus pulled up at the stop and she had to move.

———

She walked away from the library. Still in shock, Beth didn't want to go to work yet—she just couldn't. She walked until she came to her favourite café: Dorian's. She ordered a hot chocolate and an almond and custard croissant. Comfort food.

The café wasn't full, so she chose the corner table at the window and sat waiting for her drink to come. Once it had, she pulled out her phone and texted Jay.

BETH: Well, he doesn't want me.

Jay replied instantly. She must have been waiting for Beth's text, after last night's conversation.

JAY: Oh, Beth, I'm so sorry!

BETH: And I've just gone
and spent my fare money.
Are you coming into town later?

JAY: Yes. I'll pick you up.
Where are you now?

BETH: Dorian's. Hot
chocolate and sweet croissant.
Feel horrible. And confused.
I feel like he's lying to me.

Beth's phone then rang in her hand. It was Jay.

"Hi Jay." Beth's voice was mouse-quiet.

"Hey, Beth. I can talk for a little while. What do you think he's lying to you about?"

"That he doesn't care about me." Beth leaned forward, angling towards the window and shielding her face from the rest of the café.

"What? You think he really does?" Jay's tone suggested she found it hard to believe.

"It's only a f…" Beth couldn't finish the last word because her throat had closed over. She covered her mouth and tried to stop any noise leaking out. She didn't want to attract attention to herself. She was shaking.

"Beth?"

Beth couldn't talk. If she talked, she would make some kind of loud noise.

"Oh dear. You're upset, aren't you? I'm so sorry," Jay said. "Okay, you sit there and drink your chocolate. Take your time. Ruby will understand. And remember: you can make up the time later."

She went on, helping Beth to carry on in the face of it all. "Get yourself together and then go to work. Distract yourself for the day and I'll pick you up out the front of the library at closing time. Text me if you need anything."

Jay waited for a moment, said, "Okay, see you later," and hung up, not waiting for a reply, which was good, as Beth was still having trouble controlling her throat.

Putting her phone away, Beth took a few deep breaths and recovered enough to take a sip of chocolate, which relaxed her throat further.

She pulled herself together, went to work and apologised to Ruby. The day was long and difficult. Somewhere between shelving returned books and scheduling in more school groups, Beth started and moaned, staring at her hand. She'd left her mother's ring on the tram. She had put it on the windowsill to moisturise her hands and left it behind when she'd dashed off.

At least Ruby hadn't asked for details. For that, Beth was grateful.

—— ELEVEN ——

At least she had other people she could talk to on the tram. All of them were kind souls and Beth took comfort in that.

The first morning after the confrontation with Isaac, she considered waiting for the next service to come, but she had to find her ring, so she showed up at the stop on time.

"Morning, Willis."

"Hello Beth. How are you today?" He was more subdued than usual.

She ignored the question. "Did anyone hand in a ring yesterday? I left it on here by mistake."

Willis frowned. "No. No, they didn't. Sorry." He gave her the ticket.

"Okay, thanks." Beth turned to find a seat—near the front.

To her relief, Tilly was sitting in the aisle seat, preventing anyone from sitting with her until Beth came.

"Come and sit with me, Beth," she said. "Those scones were delicious." She moved into the window seat and Beth took her place. Beth was amused when Tilly gave her back the plastic bag she'd given her the scone in. Instead of using the zip-lock opening, Tilly had torn a hole in the side of it.

Funny old Tilly.

They chatted away about scone-making again, Tilly telling her, "Be sure to keep everything as cold as you can—even your hands. And mix it as little as possible." She would have to cook some more.

Beth kept her head and upper body facing Tilly as she talked. She would ignore anyone who might need a seat. Today, she wanted to spend this time with a friend.

Her stop in the city came far too soon and, despite the roiling snakes in her stomach, Beth got up and moved to the back door. Isaac was sitting in his usual seat. He was aware of her, but he didn't look up.

As the door opened, she spoke his name. He looked up, his eyes narrow. "Did you see my ring on the windowsill yesterday?" she asked quickly.

He paused for an instant and looked down. "No."

Once again, Beth got the impression he was lying to her. Pounding down the steps, she flung herself off the tram and strode to work.

What the hell? Is he a thief as well?

After a couple of hours brooding over the situation, Beth concluded she must be inept at reading body language. And she'd put Maxine down for not knowing about it. What a hypocrite. Perhaps she'd better re-read the books she'd recommended to Maxine.

Because of her splurge on comfort food the previous morning—two tram rides' worth—Beth had to find the cash for another fare before her next payday. She would have to use part of the amount she'd been saving for a new winter jacket and put off buying it for another week or two. She got the cash out of the envelope she kept in her lockable desk drawer and asked the cashier to give her some change for it.

Beth's trips to and from work became awkward and

uncomfortable. She avoided Isaac as much as she could and got to know Tilly, Willis and Margie even more. Fortunately, Isaac stayed down the back.

Two weeks later, she saw Maxine again. She looked elegant, as before. In fact—Beth had to look twice—she was practically wearing the exact same outfit, down to the prissy umbrella.

Beth avoided her.

Margie always had some treat or other in her basket, fresh and warm. Beth kept drawing her out and discovering more about her, in little bite-sized pieces.

She tried out more of Tilly's cooking and baking suggestions and, whenever she could, she brought some of it in to share with her, Margie and Willis. She showed Tilly how to open the plastic bag the right way.

At the end of one particularly long day, full of school groups and tours, Beth got on the tram and had to stand for most of the ride. Her feet were already sore from standing all day, so when she noticed a vacant seat, about halfway down, she headed for it.

It was only while she was sitting down she realised her seatmate was the older man who had glared at Isaac. Far from feeling intimidated by him, however, she was curious.

"Hello, I'm Beth." She stuck out her hand.

His eyebrows rose and he inhaled sharply before he introduced himself. "Good afternoon, Beth. I'm Gareth." His tone was polite—and not unfriendly. He had an accent Beth couldn't pick. Irish? Yorkshire?

"Gareth. It's nice to meet you."

He smiled and then Beth saw the hand she was shaking. It was wrapped in a bandage.

"What happened to your hand?" she asked, letting go in case she was hurting him.

He looked down at it. "Ah, yes. I'm a gardener. I did myself some mischief with the secateurs." His voice was deep.

"You're a gardener?" Beth commented, "My grandparents used to be great gardeners. My grandmother taught me a little. Mostly how to weed." Beth tilted her head at Gareth and smiled wryly.

Gareth chuckled. "Yes. An important skill," he said.

Beth asked him straight out, "Do you know Isaac Lyttelton?"

The question took him by surprise. He paused and looked sideways at her. "Yes."

Beth was amazed at how blunt she was being. "You looked angry at him a few weeks ago. Are you…" She searched for the right word. "Are you enemies? Rivals?"

Gareth's face relaxed. "Neither. We were having a disagreement at the time." He added, "We're friends. He's a good man." He was nodding. "But prone to making mistakes—as we all are."

Beth appreciated his candour. She was thankful Jay had talked her into finding out the real situation but didn't feel up to forgiving Isaac just yet.

"How do you know him? Do you live at the end of the line, too?" she asked.

"I'm employed by him," said Gareth.

"Oh, of course. The properties need gardening. Where are…"

He interrupted her. "I think this is your stop." He was pointing out the window.

"Oh, thank you." She jumped up. "I'm always doing that. See you later," she called over her shoulder as she dashed for the door.

Hang on! How did he know this was my stop?

She reported the new information to Jay when she got home. Beth was glad to have someone to share these things with.

Jay shook her head at Beth. "You're so forward. I wouldn't dare introduce myself to someone and then ask them a question like that."

Beth shrugged.

"But Beth," Jay's eyes lit up. "I need to go into town tomorrow morning so I'll be joining you on the tram."

"Yeah? Fantastic!" Beth was glad she would be able to introduce Jay to her new friends. But her gladness was tainted by the situation with Isaac. If only...

Nope. No point in going there.

———

The next morning they stood at the stop together, having arrived in good time, and waited for everyone else to get on before mounting the steps to Willis.

"Hello, Willis," said Beth. "This is my flatmate, Jay."

Willis beamed at her. "Good morning, Jay. What a pleasure to meet you. And what a lovely flatmate you have."

Jay grinned. "She's been telling me all about you."

"Well, don't believe everything you hear." Willis winked at her.

Jay tittered and she and Beth went on a search for empty seats. They found only one—next to Tilly. Beth got Jay to sit in it and stood in the aisle, putting her bag at Jay's feet. She then introduced her to Tilly and Margie, who was in the seat behind.

Margie offered them both a baked treat.

As she munched on it, Beth commented, "Your baking's always fresh, Margie, and even a little warm, too. How do you do that?"

All Margie did was smile and say, "Oh ho, you sweet girl," in her rolling accent.

Beth looked for Isaac then, out of habit, and found him

already gazing at her. She stopped breathing. Ridiculous hope made her maintain the connection but before long Isaac looked away, his head dipping down.

Rattled, Beth turned back to her friends, swallowing hard, and caught Margie's shy gaze, warm and full of what looked like regret. She gave Beth a small smile.

Tilly asked Jay what she did and Beth busied herself showed Tilly and Margie the photos of Jay's art pieces she had on her phone.

They were almost at the depot when Beth said, "You must watch what Willis does here, Jay."

Her friend looked out the window. Fortunately, no one was in the way, so she didn't have to stand up. Beth explained what Willis had told her about the procedure of turning the tram and what little she'd discovered in the books she'd found about it.

"Doesn't he make it look easy?" said Beth, as Willis leaned against the post and the tram spun around. Jay watched, making no comment.

Beth was shoved from behind. The bullyboys were pushing past, only three of them this time, trying to get to the back of the tram. She glared at them as they passed and then tapped Jay's shoulder and whispered, "There are those boys I told you about."

Jay continued to stare out the window at Willis. Beth wondered why she was ignoring her.

"Jay?"

Tilly spoke suddenly, "Beth dear. I nearly forgot. I got my oven to work last night at home and I managed to bake some of my old scones. I meant to bring some this morning, but…" She paused, then carried on in a rush, her eyes wide. "But I had some unexpected guests and they ate them all. I must try to do some more for you."

The tram moved forward on its journey to town and Jay then turned her head back to the front.

"Isn't it interesting, Jay? I'd never seen it before I rode on this. Have you?" said Beth.

Jay looked up at her, her eyebrows knitted together. "What?"

Tilly interrupted again. "I must say they were just as I remembered them. Quite good, they were, quite good." She then looked behind her. "Do you remember those, Margie?" She was being quite loud, to Beth's amusement.

"Oh, yes, Tilly, I certainly do," bubbled Margie, far more animated than usual. "They were bonnie scones, they were. You must taste them, Beth, dear."

"My granny used to make fabulous scones," Jay announced. "She would put lemonade in them. It made them fluffy."

"Lemonade?" Tilly looked astonished. "What a strange thing to put in scones."

Jay laughed. "I know, but it worked well. The carbonation puts a lot more air in them." She looked up at Beth. "I should make some for you, then you can bring them in for these two."

Beth grinned down at her. "Yeah, absolutely. That'd be fantastic." She noticed Tilly and Margie exchange an odd look.

When Jay and Beth got off, they used the back door so Jay could see Isaac, as he was sitting in his usual place, behind the back door.

"Huh," said Jay, once the door had shut. "He looked really sad. Otherwise I would have stopped and told him off, you know."

Beth stared at Jay. "Oh, lord, I'm glad you didn't. That would have been so embarrassing."

They walked towards the library and Beth said to Jay, "So now you've seen the tram and the people I've been going on about since I moved in. You'll know who I'm talking about now."

"Yeah," said Jay. "But you forgot to show me where the tram gets turned around. I would've liked to have seen that."

Beth stopped and took Jay by the elbow. "What are you talking about?" she said. "I did show you. You were looking at it the whole time."

Jay frowned at Beth and shook her head. "No. I didn't see a thing."

"But…" Beth couldn't believe what she was hearing. "But you were looking out the window at the time. I pointed it out to you."

Jay's head retracted and she looked at Beth, a blank look on her face.

Beth stood, staring at Jay. She opened her mouth to object but closed it again, shrugged and carried on walking, shaking her head.

"That is so weird," she said as Jay caught up. "I distinctly remember pointing it out to you. And then dear Tilly was rabbiting on about scones." She was finding it difficult not to be annoyed at Jay for not paying attention.

"Sorry," muttered Jay. "I remember us talking about scones, though. I'll make some tonight, eh?" she said.

—— TWELVE ——

One day at work, Beth came across a sixty-year-old map of the city. She looked up her suburb and found the street she lived on to see if it'd changed much. She discovered she lived in one of the older parts of the city and it looked about the same. But also on the map were marks showing the bus and tram routes and she saw how close the end of the tram line was to where she and Jay lived. There was even a pedestrian shortcut.

She'd been getting curious about what was at the end of the line, so she decided, since the weather was so good and the sun was still setting well after she got home, she would pay a visit to where her friends lived. She would look around and then walk home.

She didn't want to put pressure on Tilly to invite her in, so she didn't mention her plan. They chatted and laughed in the balmy late afternoon.

That was, until they got to Beth's usual stop.

Willis called out first, "Here's your stop, Beth." They all knew how distracted she got.

Beth leaned out into the aisle and found his reflection in

the mirror. "I'm staying on a bit longer, Willis. Don't worry about me."

He looked perplexed, but he closed the doors and drove on.

Tilly asked her where she was going.

"I'm going to come to the end to see where the tram goes." She went on, trying to make light of it. "I've been curious about it for a while and I came across an old map in the library today and I saw how close it is to where Jay and I live. The sun's going down late these days so I'll have plenty of light to get home safely. I'll walk around and then head back."

Tilly's smile looked strained. "Oh, love, there's nothing to see down there. It's only houses and little flats," she said.

"But I want to see," repeated Beth, shrugging. She heard footsteps behind her.

Tilly leaned towards her and put her hand on her knee. "Dear Beth, I can't invite you in, darling." She was whispering.

Damn! Tilly's freaking out. Exactly what I didn't want.

Beth put her hand on Tilly's in turn and shook her head. "No, no, don't worry. I wasn't expecting you to. No pressure. I'm only going to walk around."

They'd halted at the next stop and a couple of people got off. Beth could hear the bullyboys laughing away down the back. Something was amusing them and they were excited about it.

The tram set off again. Beth kept looking around at the new sights to see. She noticed Gareth was sitting on the other side of the aisle from her. He was peering at her, a slight frown on his face.

She grinned and waved at him. The smile that followed looked a bit forced. Funny man. She must spend another trip with him, see what he was all about.

A big laugh rolled up from the boys at the back. Gareth's

eyes flicked back and faced the front again.

Then came the penultimate stop. Willis halted the tram and opened the doors and one more person got off.

Tilly spoke quickly then. "Dear Beth, don't bother with the end of the line, dear. There's nothing to see. Go home, now. You don't want to go there. There's nothing."

Her insistence was puzzling.

They hadn't moved from the stop and the doors were still open. Beth saw Willis looking at her in the mirror. He then put on what she assumed was the handbrake, flipped open his little barrier and stood up.

He walked over to her. "Beth, love, you have to get off now."

Beth couldn't believe it. "Why?"

"Come on, now," said Willis. He even took her hand and pulled. "You have to get off. Because..." He paused for a moment and then smiled grimly. "Because only the residents can go farther than this stop." He nodded.

Beth, frowning, allowed him to pull her to her feet, but he didn't get her to the door. She stopped at the driver's seat.

"Surely you could ignore that for once," she said, "I'm not going to do anything. I'm just going to walk around, see the place, and then walk home," Beth pleaded with him. This was too strange.

He stood and looked at her for a while and then checked his watch—which significantly changed his demeanour. He became brisk.

"Now, Beth, I've got a timetable to keep to. Best get going, love. Quick, now." He flapped his hands as if she were a bad smell he was trying to push out.

"This doesn't make sense." Beth shook her head at him. "Is someone going to arrest me? This is ridiculous." She sat down again in the nearest seat. "You drive on, Willis..."

She was interrupted by Isaac's voice.

"Beth," he said loudly. She looked back. He was sitting with Margie, right behind Tilly. His arms were folded and he was leaning back in his seat.

He tilted his head at her. "I don't know why you should be so interested in a place where you're not wanted. For crying out loud: stop holding us up and go home, girl," he drawled, and she could swear she saw a sneer on his face.

The boys down the back guffawed.

"Fine," said Beth, her eyes stinging. She could feel her face on fire as she scuttled down the steps and onto the pavement. She looked up the stairs at Willis, who looked relieved and concerned in equal measure. He'd followed her partway down the steps.

Humiliated, she told him off. "This is complete—"

But then the door closed in her face. Eyes wide, she drew her head back at the last second, to stop it hitting her.

She saw Willis swing around and jump back up the steps towards the driver's chair, and even before he got to it, the tram pulled away from the stop.

They were all in a hurry to leave her.

Beth stared up at the tram as it passed her. She saw Gareth get out of his seat and head for the other side of the tram. Along with the bullyboys up the back, one more person sat on the tram: a woman with a hat. Was that Maxine?

She kept watching until the tram disappeared around the next corner, thinking about what Isaac had said. Why had he been so cruel? A lump formed in her throat. She swallowed it.

"Bugger that!" she muttered.

Beth walked towards where she'd last seen the tram. She was going to follow it and she was going to tell that man exactly what she thought of him.

She arrived at the corner. The stop couldn't be too far

ahead. She wasn't sure how far, though, so she followed the overhead tramline.

When the tramline stopped a few hundred metres up the road, Beth stopped too. No tram. Had she missed a side road? She searched the area and then doubled back to find the turnoff.

But there was none.

What?

"Are you lost?" said a voice behind her.

She whirled around, startled. A lean, grubby-looking man stood at his garden gate. He wore only a singlet and baggy pants, feet bare. His sudden appearance was disturbing and Beth felt suddenly unsafe.

But the sun was still up. She would be fine.

"Where's the tram?" she asked.

"Tram? What tram?" His voice was slurred.

She pointed down the road. "The tram I was on," she said clearly. "I got off around the corner and it came this way and now it's gone. Where did it go?"

He leered at her. "You're a bit drunk, aren't you, sweetie?" He laughed, "Fhaa-haa-haa! There's been no trams for years now. Why don't you come inside?"

Beth insisted, her voice rising in pitch. "But I was just on one. I wasn't imagining things. And no, I am not drunk."

He shrugged. "Well, we haven't had trams on these roads for decades. My mum used to talk about them from when she was a kid."

Beth pointed up to the overhead line. "So what's that doing there?" She was fuming, with Isaac having got away, and her fuse was already short. This guy had better watch it.

The man looked up at where she pointed. "Oh, they haven't bothered getting rid of it, that's all. Probably costs too much money, the tightwads."

Beth peered up at the line. It did look pretty old and rusty, but she couldn't believe she'd imagined being on a tram. Not all this time. How was that possible?

She threw up her hands. "Fine. Thanks." Shaking her head, she walked towards the alley that would take her back home.

"No worries," he replied. "Do ya wanna come in for a drink?"

Beth threw a look over her shoulder. "No thanks. I want to go home."

She carried on walking, hoping he wouldn't ask again.

———

"Isaac said *what*?" Jay had stopped what she was doing once Beth had got home and begun ranting about what had just happened.

"'Why do you want to go to a place where you're not wanted?'" Beth recited. The phrase had played over and over in her head all the way back home. "It was heartless. I never would have expected it. I never thought he was a cruel man." She looked at Jay. "Perhaps it's best he's not interested." She'd been struggling with that stupid lump in her throat since he'd said it.

"Well, I hope you give him a piece of your mind the next time you see him," said Jay. The heat in her voice made the lump return with a vengeance and Beth had to swallow and swallow. She looked away.

Jay stepped towards her, and flung her arms around her. "Oh, Beth! I'm so sorry. We really had our hopes up, didn't we? He seemed so nice."

Beth held on, but couldn't hold back her tears. "I'm so glad you told me to find out what he wanted. And what he didn't." Her voice was small. She swallowed again. "It's clear now, isn't it?"

Jay pulled back and looked Beth in the face. "Would you

like me to cook dinner tonight? Then you could relax."

Beth considered. It was a heartfelt offer and Beth knew Jay meant it for the best, but she declined. "No thanks, Jay. Really. I've got dinner all planned and it'll keep me busy. I need busy right now."

Jay nodded. "You let me know if I can help."

"Actually," Beth said, "that'd be nice. If you're in the kitchen, I can rattle on at you. It might help. Is that okay?"

Jay grinned at her. "Absolutely!" But her face changed then and she pointed at Beth. "And if I ever come across that man again, I am gonna tell him exactly what I think of him."

Wiping her face, Beth smiled at her friend's fervent declaration of support.

———

It wasn't only Isaac who had hurt Beth's feelings. The words and actions of Tilly and Willis played through her mind during the long hours of the night. Had they meant to be mean? She couldn't believe they had. The whole thing didn't make sense. She wasn't looking forward to going to work in the morning.

Should she catch an earlier service? Or a later one? No. She didn't want to be late to work and catching the earlier one meant she would have to wander around the city for at least half an hour before the library opened. The tram always arrived right on time for her to get to work.

Well, perhaps she should avoid them and sit somewhere else. But it would be hard to avoid Willis. After a little while, she concluded he'd only been doing his job. At least he'd looked sorry.

Unlike Isaac.

Beth replayed what he'd said, and how he'd said it, over and over in her mind. The sneer on his face, his arms folded.

How he'd been so arrogantly sprawled on the seat.

Okay, she'd misunderstood his signals. But it didn't give him the right to be so nasty. Well, she was already managing to avoid him so she wouldn't have to do much more.

Jerk!

As it was, she slept through her alarm the next morning and almost missed the tram anyway. She just managed to catch it, racing up the front steps, the last one on.

"Morning, Beth, love," said Willis. He leaned towards her, his voice low. "I'm so sorry about last night. Can you forgive me?" He looked so contrite; how could she not? The apology made her eyes threaten tears. Dear Willis!

She nodded and smiled. She was breathing hard.

"Look, you get yourself together and pay at the end." He pointed his thumb behind him. "Tilly's waiting for you."

Beth started down the aisle. Dear Tilly. She was standing in the aisle and holding out her arm to guide Beth into the window seat. She looked apologetic, too.

Beth avoided looking for Isaac. She didn't want to see him. But she couldn't see much anyway, what with tears threatening. She sat down and Tilly took over the aisle seat.

"Oh, I'm so sorry, dear," said Tilly. "We should have told you about the rules. We didn't mean to embarrass you." She wrapped Beth's hand in both of hers, her dry skin warm and tissue-thin.

Beth nodded. "I was hurt by it, but I'll be fine—as long as I don't have to talk to Isaac ever again."

Tilly's face sank but she nodded. "I understand, dear."

"Have you made any scones for me?" joked Beth, looking wistfully at Tilly.

Tilly chuckled. "Oh, no, dear. I wish I had."

"Here, Beth, have one of these," said Margie, right behind them, as usual. She proffered her basket and Beth took a delicious-looking pastry.

"Thanks, Margie," said Beth. She took a bite. Still warm.

Tilly squeezed her hand and leaned towards her. "I do enjoy talking with you, Beth. You're such a lovely, bright, generous young lady. You make my day, you know?" And now Tilly's eyes teared up. Beth patted her hand.

Tilly swallowed. "Alright, my dear. Just a minute." She closed her eyes and took in a breath. "And forgive me."

She let go of Beth's hand and stood up. Stepping down the aisle a little, she revealed Isaac sitting across from them. Beth's mouth dropped open, her eyes widening.

He was the last person she wanted to talk to. Nevertheless, over the aisle he came and he sat down beside Beth, who shrank away from him and pointedly looked out the window, taking another bite of the pastry, though her appetite had disappeared. The blood drained from her face.

Out of the corner of her eye, she saw Tilly sit down where Isaac had been sitting.

What the hell?

They sat in a long silence and Beth seriously considered jumping up and leaving these strange, strange people to their little, freaky dance.

Isaac sighed. "Elizabeth?"

Somehow, this one word reached into Beth's soul and made it jangle so hard she gasped.

Damn my treacherous heart!

"I am so very sorry for what I said," he continued, as Beth took a deep, shaky breath and continued to stare out the window.

His voice sounded strained. "I can't explain why I spoke to you in such a…" He took a deep breath himself. "In such a despicable manner. I know I hurt you. If I could erase those moments out of your memory, I would."

Beth didn't know how to respond. He sounded like he meant it, but his demeanour last night had been so callous. She didn't know what to believe.

He went on. "Dearest Beth. I have more to beg your forgiveness for. I've misled you—right from the beginning."

Beth frowned. What did he mean?

"Your presence in my life," he said, "was so unexpectedly precious, so full of delight. Every moment I spent with you was utterly extraordinary."

What?

"I couldn't get enough of you. When I wasn't with you, I ached for your presence. When I couldn't speak with you, I yearned to hear your voice."

This made Beth's insides flip-flop. Today he was saying all the right things. But yesterday…

This just isn't fair!

Isaac's voice was low, but he was leaning towards her and she could feel his warm breath on her neck as he continued. "But I tried to convince myself we were only friends, that what I felt was merely platonic in nature." He sighed again, making her hair tickle her throat. "I deceived myself, and in so doing, I trifled with your feelings. I hope you can find it in your heart to forgive me."

After a long pause, he went on. "And now I will tell you the truth. While I can." She heard him swallow. "My feelings for you, dearest, sweet Beth, are…" He stopped and wet his lips. "are… profound." He took a deep breath. "And far from platonic."

Beth finally turned to him, lightheaded. His face was so close to hers, his eyes so blue, she couldn't help but believe him, caught within some spell he cast, perhaps. But, for some reason, his expression was sad.

"If I were free to," he whispered, as he enfolded her

hand in both of his. "I would spend my life… making your acquaintance."

Beth's eyes grew wide.

Does that mean what I think it means?

Isaac carried on.

"But…" He shook his head. "to my everlasting regret, I am not free." He swallowed.

The bullyboys at the back chose this moment to burst into cackling laughter that went on and on. Isaac's face stiffened, his eyes fell from hers, and he clamped his teeth together.

Something made Beth look towards the rear of the tram, towards the boys who were still rocking in amusement, and then back to Isaac. A niggle of a suspicion tickled the back of her mind.

"What is going on here?" she asked.

The boys stopped laughing.

Isaac's eyes met hers again, then widened. He drew in his breath as he straightened in the seat. Releasing her hand, he set both of his on his knees, his head bowed. He seemed frozen in place.

Tilly leaned over the aisle, speaking quickly. "I hope we can continue to be friends, dear. You've brought us such joy. And you, bringing in your baking, it's been delicious. Thank you. Thank you so much."

Beth saw Gareth on the other side of her, also looking at Beth. He still had a bandage on his hand. Hadn't that cut healed yet?

She felt Margie's hand on her shoulder and a short squeeze. Beth had forgotten the pastry in her hand.

Looking up, she found Willis watching her in the mirror, between keeping his eyes on the road. He smiled when their eyes met, his eyebrows raised.

This was such a strange predicament. Beth didn't know

what to make of it. Isaac had told her he wanted to *make her acquaintance*, for crying out loud.

But he couldn't.

Why?

"This is really strange," she said.

"I know." More relaxed now, Isaac cleared his throat as he nodded. "But now I hope, since I've finally been honest with you, we can resume our friendship." He studied her face then, his eyes pleading. "I've hated having you avoid me these last few weeks."

Beth stopped before answering. She wasn't sure how she should react.

"We'll see," she said finally. "I'm still reeling from all this. First yesterday… now today." She looked up at him. "What am I supposed to think, Isaac?" She shook her head. "You're going to have to give me some time."

He let his breath out in a long exhale. "I understand." He reached into the breast pocket of his jacket, closed his eyes and opened them again. "I have another confession." He couldn't look her in the eye.

Another one?

"I kept this," he said. "To remember you by."

He held out his hand. On the tip of his index finger was her mother's ring.

Beth stared at it a moment before she took the ring and put it back on her finger. The ring was warm from his breast pocket. She was left speechless.

Willis called out, "Beth, love. This is your stop."

Beth moved into automatic. She put the remains of the pastry into her mouth and it dissolved as she gathered her things together.

Isaac stood to let her out, his eyes playing over her face as she passed him.

She hadn't paid yet. She took out her purse, opened the coin pouch and pulled out a handful of coins. Opening her hand, she found another crusted, ancient coin amongst them.

"Willis, I've got some more funny money. You take it, don't you?" Her voice sounded distant and distracted.

She put the regular coins in the wooden bowl and held out the antique one to Willis. But when she looked up, she found his face had gone chalky white.

"Are you alright? What's wrong?" Beth froze in place, alarmed. He wasn't having a heart attack, was he?

Willis swallowed and nodded. "Yep, I'm fine, love. Just a bit of a sore back." He picked up the change and gave her a ticket. He looked like he was tasting something bitter.

Beth turned to bid her friends farewell and was startled to find Isaac standing right behind her, gazing at her face, as if trying to memorise it.

Shocked by how close he was, she pulled away. "Well, see you tonight, then," she said, and started down the steps.

"Goodbye, Beth." Isaac's voice was solemn and final, and his tone made her look up at him in puzzlement once she'd hit the pavement.

He was deathly pale as he clutched a pole and both he and Willis were gazing at her, their faces drawn.

What is wrong with them?

Glad to be getting out of such an odd situation, Beth waved at them, smiling, trying to lift the mood.

No response.

The door shut and the tram moved away, leaving Beth with a feeling of dread.

What the heck just happened?

———

As soon as Beth got to work—she was early—she sat in the empty workroom and called Jay, who answered straight away.

"Hey, Beth."

"You okay to chat for a minute?" Beth asked.

"Yeah, absolutely." Jay sounded keen to hear.

Beth shook her head to herself, still not believing it. "I just had the weirdest trip into town." When she finished the story, there was an extended silence.

"Jay," she said finally. "Is it just me, or is that seriously wacky?"

"No, it's not just you," Jay said. "That's one of the strangest things I've ever heard. What are you going to do?"

"I don't know," said Beth.

—— THIRTEEN ——

His feelings for her were *profound*. That's what he'd said.

"That goes on the 'pro' side," Beth muttered. She stopped and her brow furrowed. "Maybe."

She was on her lunch break later the same day and still struggling with the morning's events. She'd taken to writing it all down to see if that would clarify matters.

She stared at her bit of paper. Currently the 'pro' side was slightly longer than the 'con' side. And her writing was getting harder to read.

At least it meant she hadn't misread his signals. So she *wasn't* abysmal at body language after all. What else had she picked up? Nasty Maxine.

And those boys... what was wrong there?

But Beth couldn't say. She just had a vague sense of something wrong.

Well, the truth was, Isaac hadn't actually asked her out. He'd said he would if he were free. But he wasn't free.

Why? What made him not free?

And what was the deal with how well these different people all knew each other? Was it because they were all from 'the end of the line'?

Which Beth had tried to visit in vain.

Where the tram had disappeared.

She had a sudden attack of goose bumps.

Beth shook her head. She had a lot of questions. She would make a list, sit with Tilly and ask them. Or Isaac.

She stopped.

Isaac. He'd deceived her. He'd lied. He'd stolen her ring, for heaven's sake! Why should she trust him? He'd told her he'd even deceived himself, that their relationship was 'platonic'. Why? Because he wasn't free?

'Free'? Why that particular word? Why not 'unavailable'? 'Not free' made it sound like he was a prisoner.

The fantastical suspicion tickled her mind again. Beth squashed it.

Don't be ridiculous!

All those long conversations she'd had with Isaac. He'd paid such close attention to her and made her feel valuable and interesting. And pretty. They'd laughed together. She pictured his keen blue eyes searching her face as she'd spoken, a smile of delight on his lips. The warmth she'd felt at the time returned to her.

And no, she hadn't imagined it. He'd told her now. He'd told her he had *profound* feelings for her. But what good was that, if he wasn't free to pursue it?

If Beth shook her head over this one more time, Ruby was sure to ask her what was wrong.

Well, she would sit and talk with Isaac, or Tilly, this afternoon on the way home. She would take her time. If he wasn't available, she had to make sure she didn't lose her heart again—if she hadn't already. This must be friendship, or she had to stay away from Isaac, for her own sake.

She felt halfway satisfied about her chosen course of action at the end of her lunch hour. She got back to work and was able to concentrate again.

Not long after lunch, Ruby came up to her.

"Are you alright?" she asked.

Beth knew she'd underperformed that morning.

"Um, yeah." She tried to make light of it. "Something really weird happened to me this morning and I've been thinking about it a lot, but it'll blow over."

"Anything you want to talk about?" asked Ruby.

"Oh, thanks, but it'll take forever to explain. I'm already talking about it with my flatmate. Thanks, though," said Beth.

Ruby folded her arms. "I have to be more careful now, asking you how you are," she said. "The last time I came up, and—in jest—asked how your head injury was, the next day you actually *had* one."

Beth looked at Ruby and remembered. "Oh, my goodness. That must have freaked you out."

Ruby nodded and broke into a wide grin.

She can't be taking it too seriously, then.

The familiar feeling of fluttering anticipation filled Beth as she stood at the stop waiting for the tram in the afternoon. It wasn't like Willis to be late. She would have to have him on about it.

She attempted to scold herself for her excitement at being able to talk to Isaac again. Yes, he'd told her he had feelings for her, but nothing could come of it. But she couldn't help herself.

You'll get yourself hurt, woman!

And this time, it would be her own damn fault.

A bus pulled up then and the people she'd been waiting with poured on to it. She stared at the bus.

A *bus*. Where was the tram?

There must be some mistake. Willis must have swapped with someone else again. Beth decided to wait for the next service, on the off chance.

Another fifteen minutes. Another bus. She had to get on anyway, or she would never get home. She would have to wait until tomorrow morning.

Damn!

She was disappointed and the bus was crowded and smelly. The exhaust from the diesel engine was somehow making its way into the cabin and it was unbearable. Beth couldn't wait to catch the tram again—quieter and cleaner.

Jay was waiting for her at home, keen to hear the news. "You're late. What happened? What did he say?"

Beth sighed. "They didn't come. I had to catch a bus. I couldn't see any of the usual people." She rubbed her temple. "I'd forgotten how much diesels stink."

The smell had given Beth a headache. Thank goodness Jay was cooking. Beth lay down to get rid of the pounding.

Beth was already exhausted from the sleepless night before, so once the headache had gone she slept well. The next morning she could relax and was in good time for the tram.

But around the corner came another diesel bus.

In order to speak to the driver, she tacked herself to the end of the line.

"What happened to the tram?" she asked him, once she'd arrived.

He squinted at her. "What are you talking about?" His tone was surprisingly aggressive.

"The tram. It's been doing this route for months. Where did it go?"

He rolled his eyes. "Why would I know?" he said. "Just

pay up and sit down!" He was wearing dangly earrings and makeup, but his expression was dour.

Beth pulled her head back. "Okay."

She paid into the automatic cash counter and the machine spat a ticket out. As she took it, she asked, "Do you know Willis?"

In response, the driver jammed his foot onto the accelerator, making her stumble down the aisle before she caught herself on one of the poles.

Gosh, he's going fast!

Beth could see the other passengers' heads jerking back and forth every time he changed gear.

Clinging to the pole, she first looked for her friends. She couldn't see them anywhere—none of them.

And then, in self-preservation, she hunted for a seat to sit in. She was going to be thrown to the floor if she had to remain standing.

The driver was rude and bullish all the way in, and his driving didn't improve one bit. Beth was sure she had whiplash by the time she got to work.

When her stop came several people were getting off at the back, so she walked to the front and braved the driver yet again.

"There are trams usually on this route, aren't there?"

He looked at her like she was insane and then barked a laugh. "Don't be stupid, woman. There haven't been trams in this city for fifty years." He looked away, shaking his head.

As she got off, he closed the door on her. He was clearly in a rush.

Beth remembered the man at the end of the line—the drunk one. He'd said pretty much the same thing. She hadn't taken notice of him, mainly because she'd been so upset, but also because he was drunk.

And Jay's friend too, ages ago.

It was Friday and she waited at the end of the day, hoping for the tram. But, once again, a diesel bus came to a stop in front of her.

The tram had to come sometime, surely. She waved the bus on and decided to wait. Two more buses passed by as she stood there. Finally, she gave up and caught the one that came over an hour after work had finished.

Once on board, Beth texted Jay—she might worry about her being so late. She searched the faces of the people on board, some of them returning her gaze with belligerence.

How could it be that none of her friends was on board? But, of course, this was the later service. Perhaps they'd been on the one at the normal time. She should have got on as usual.

Beth berated herself all the way home. She was expecting them to always be on the tram. That was daft. They could just as easily be on a bus.

Perhaps Willis was sick. Perhaps he *had* been having a heart attack. The thought made Beth's innards go cold. And, she realised, there was no way for anyone to let her know.

Right. From now on she would catch her regular services and at some point she would see her friends again. And, when she did, she must get someone's phone number—a landline at least.

Jay was waiting for her, eager to hear what'd happened and disappointed when nothing had. They had leftovers for dinner.

The weekend was going to be endless. It felt like Monday was aeons away. Beth had to fill in the time somehow, so she decided to do some online research during some of the long hours until Monday.

She looked up the buses and trams for the city.

"It says here," she said to Jay, who was sitting at her workbench nearby. "It says they stopped using trams in 1964."

Jay looked at her and shook her head. "But…" She didn't finish; she looked stunned.

"But we both went on a tram," Beth finished for her. "You went on a tram, right?"

At this point, Beth needed to check she hadn't lost her mind.

"Yes. Absolutely, I did." Jay was nodding. "It was gorgeous. All wooden, one line overhead, running on tracks. That's a tram, isn't it?"

"Yes," Beth replied. "Apparently it has one overhead line because the full circuit's made using the track. And that is the definition of a tram."

"So, were we both hallucinating?" asked Jay. But she spoke again, without waiting for Beth's answer. "Didn't someone tell me there were no more trams here, like, ages ago? I texted you."

"Yeah, you did. Then I asked you what you'd given me for breakfast, for me to hallucinate all the way to work."

"Yeah, that's right." Jay smiled at the memory. Then her face darkened. "So what the dickens is going on?"

Beth searched for an explanation. "I wonder if perhaps they were low on buses for some reason and they got one of the old trams out to compensate. They were saying in the news a while ago they were low on resources."

Jay nodded. "Well, it's a possibility. But, surely they wouldn't have had a tram in good enough condition to use straight away."

Beth looked further down the web page. What she saw made her frown. "Okay, that's even weirder. None of the photos on here look remotely like the tram we caught."

Jay got up and came over to see, and then agreed. "They

look completely different." She added, "I liked the pretty light fittings on the ceiling. They were elegant."

"Oh yeah."

Jay bent over to look again at the photos online. "So, mystery upon mystery," she said.

"I wonder if Willis would know. I should ask him when I see him," said Beth.

"Great idea." Jay straightened. "When you see him."

She sounded more than a little doubtful.

———

And, it turned out, she was right to doubt. After what felt like the longest weekend Beth could ever remember, she was forced to catch a diesel bus to work again. No Willis, no Tilly, no Margie, certainly no Isaac.

Her heart felt like it was shrinking as she did her best to text Jay the news while being flung back and forth by the angry driver. The dangly earrings had changed, but his outlook on life hadn't. Beth didn't bother asking him any more questions.

Perhaps her trip home would be more fruitful.

But, once again, a bus pulled up at the stop and, once again, none of her friends were aboard. At least this driver didn't drive like a complete maniac.

The next morning was the same, much to Beth's frustration. She braced herself against the window of the seat she found and stared out, holding on to the back of the seat in front of her, so she wouldn't be thrown around so much as they jerked through the suburbs.

She saw the bridge coming up. They hadn't passed through the depot this time. Perhaps only the tram had to pass through it.

That would explain how empty it'd seemed, if they didn't

use many trams.

She was late to work again, as she'd been the day before, which was ironic, considering the behaviour of the driver. She considered using the earlier service. Perhaps she should call the bus company and put in a complaint.

But the main frustration was the disappearance of her friends—particularly Isaac. She desperately wanted to see them again. And their disappearance didn't even make sense.

She decided to see if she could get any information out of the driver in the afternoon. Being one of the last on a crammed bus, she was close to him, at least.

"Hello," she said. "Am I allowed to speak to you?"

The traffic was dense, so he had to maintain his concentration, but he replied, "Oh, yeah. What about?"

"The bus services." Beth went on, "I catch the 8:15 service in the morning and this one in the afternoon. Until recently, the service was running a tram and I was wondering where it'd gone."

The driver glanced at her. "A tram? No, no, we don't have trams here. Was it a smaller bus or something?"

Beth frowned. "No, I don't think so. It had one overhead wand connecting to the electricity and it ran on rails. That's a tram, isn't it?"

"Yeah, but…" He stopped talking as he negotiated a set of lights. "But we don't have any trams here at all. The only ones are in the museum. They were all taken out years ago."

"That's really strange," was all Beth could say in response. The back of her neck prickled.

"Well," he said. "I could have a chat to the dispatcher, see whether they were using some other kind of vehicle. I'll be doing this shift for a few more days, so if you catch this one again, you'll see me."

"That'd be great, thanks. What's your name?" she asked.

"Gary."

"Thanks, Gary." And then Beth had to move down the bus.

Gary came back the next day with the news that there definitely hadn't been a tram running. Anywhere. He pointed out that the city no longer had tracks set into the road, so no trams could run anyway.

Why hadn't she noticed that?

Am I losing my mind?

By the end of two weeks with no sign of any of her friends, Beth was losing hope. And her suspicions were increasing.

She spent more time on the computer at home the next Saturday. Jay suggested she look up Isaac's name on the internet. It didn't take long for her to eliminate those with images attached and there wasn't much left after that.

Later that morning she remembered he'd been educated in Cambridge. She wondered if they had records of past students available online. Happily, she discovered an over-arching database for all of the colleges of Cambridge, with an easy-to-use search engine.

She entered Isaac's name and guessed the years he would have studied. But no one came up. She broadened the year range, but still nothing. Had he been lying about that as well?

Perhaps she had his name wrong. She tried a few different spelling variations. No luck.

Going back to the original spelling, Beth saw a button she hadn't noticed before, right next to the 'Search' button: Advanced Search. She moved the cursor to select it, but accidentally pressed 'Search' instead. And she hadn't put the years in yet. She clicked on the Stop button a few times, but the search went through anyway. She rolled her eyes at her own incompetence.

I must need lunch.

But the search returned an entry: Isaac Gordon Francis

Lyttelton was awarded a Bachelors Degree in Classics and Arts.

There he is!

She breathed a long sigh. He did exist.

But then she saw the year: 1905. Beth's insides felt like they were trying to curl up inside her.

"Jay!" Her voice was a squeak. She cleared her throat. "Jay, look at this. Am I mad?"

Jay got up from her workbench and came over. "What?"

Beth pointed at the screen. Jay read the entry out loud. Her reaction was underwhelming. "Oh, that must be one of his ancestors."

Of course! That's what it is.

Beth laughed at herself, shaking her head.

"What?" said Jay.

"I've got so freaked out about how he's disappeared, I immediately thought…" She smiled up at Jay. "I thought it was actually him. You know, with his old-fashioned manners and because he didn't have a phone or anything. Mad woman. Gosh, I've got to get myself some lunch." She felt her face flushing.

While she was heating soup up for the two of them, Beth gently pressed her fingers into the back of her neck. It was stiff from craning forward to peer at the screen. She needed to spend some time away from the computer.

She proposed they go for a walk after lunch. Jay was keen, so they walked through to the supposed end of the line.

Beth pointed up. "That's where the overhead line ends. I walked back and forth looking for the tram and couldn't figure out how it had disappeared."

They followed the line the entire way and, again, found no turn off.

"That's weird," said Jay.

Beth felt much better for some fresh air and food. She

settled back into the home office chair and re-entered Isaac's name in the Cambridge search engine. She would start from the beginning so she could make sure she hadn't made a silly error somewhere.

It confirmed an Isaac Gordon Francis Lyttelton, BA in Classics and Arts in 1905.

Perhaps she should do a general search on him, now she had his full name. It might spit up some information to help her find her Isaac.

'My' Isaac? The man's not available—don't get too attached!

She copied down the name, went to one of the genealogy websites and typed it in. Taking a few seconds to process, the site then presented one option to her.

It didn't give her many details, but listed a lot of associated attachments. His date of death was 1914. He must have died in the war.

She clicked on 'Family Tree' and it proceeded to map out his ancestors. He was an only child and had no children.

Damn. A dead end.

Though it couldn't possibly be the right person, Beth clicked on the photo attached to the family tree out of interest.

To her surprise, the man pictured looked exactly like Isaac. He must be his ancestor, after all. How strange.

But then Beth looked at the other person in the photo. What she saw made her entire body go cold.

"Jay." This time her voice was low and shaky. It was all she could manage. She pointed at the screen.

Jay looked at Beth with a frown before coming over. She examined the photo.

"So, it is his ancestor, then?" she said, "Gosh, he does look like your Isaac, doesn't he?"

"Jay," Beth said again and then swallowed. She felt sick. She pointed at the woman standing next to him. "That's Maxine."

Jay froze for a moment. "What?"

The caption said: "Lord Isaac Lyttelton and his fiancée, Lady Maxine Mandeville, January 1914." Beth's pulse was racing.

Please, please, Jay, explain this away!

Jay, however, looked as lost as Beth felt.

"Are you sure?" she asked, her voice small.

Beth looked again. "As sure as I can be. But it's not possible, so how?"

"Well," Jay's eyes widened and she stepped back. "Keep looking. Don't jump to conclusions. It's insane, anyway." She backed away and flapped her hand towards the computer as she went back to her workbench. "Keep looking."

Beth did keep looking, but what she found didn't help her. Discovering the Isaac in the picture was a lord made it easier to find him though. Better records were kept for the nobility.

She came across another photo of Maxine. Yes, it still looked like Maxine.

Jay abandoned her own work and came over to sit with Beth at the desk.

The next photo they found was a group photo of the Lyttelton household: butlers, footmen, ladies' maids, valets and more. A large group. Lord Lyttelton stood behind his mother who was sitting in the centre, stiff and tall, on an elegant chair. Around them stood their staff.

"Oh, my goodness," Beth moaned. She covered her mouth.

"What?"

Beth pointed to a woman standing with the maids on the left hand side, her hair in a bun, her outline generous. "There's Margie."

Jay bent in close and then, mouth open, looked wide-eyed at Beth. She recognised her, too.

Beth searched the other faces. "And there's Gareth. And

Willis. And Tilly." Her finger moved around the photo on the screen.

She examined the photo's caption. Gareth was listed as the gardener. He'd said he was a gardener.

She looked further. "Margie's the cook. Tilly was a tenant's wife, it says." The list of names was long. "And Willis." She shook her head in disbelief. "He's their driver."

She noticed she'd used mixed tenses to describe them as she pointed at each one. Was it 'is' or 'was'?

Jay and Beth sat staring at the photo for a long time.

"I don't know what to do with this information," Beth said. "I don't know how to…" She broke off. "What am I supposed to do?"

Jay looked at Beth. "You said he died. You said Isaac died in 1914."

"In the war?" Beth's chest constricted, she had to struggle to continue. "He died in the First World War?"

"Did he? You don't sound certain," Jay pointed out.

Beth swallowed her distress. Jay was right: she'd only seen a year of death and assumed it was due to the war.

They dug deeper into Isaac's life and discovered he hadn't died in the war. They found a newspaper article, taken from May 1914—two months before the war began. It said he'd disappeared, along with several of his household, and hadn't been seen since the week before. They'd printed a photograph in the hopes someone would recognise him and report his whereabouts.

The two flatmates continued the search in the newspaper archives and found one follow-up article, a few months later in December. Isaac hadn't been found. He was still missing and was presumed dead and so were those who disappeared with him. It was a great mystery.

Jay put her hand on Beth's arm. She spoke gently. "Do you

think, perhaps, we met a group of... ghosts?"

Beth sat for a moment, thinking about what that would imply.

"It means..." Beth's voice broke and she had to stop. Jay squeezed her arm. Beth took several deep, shaking breaths past her constricted throat.

"It means he's dead," she squeaked out.

Her Isaac. So warm. Such blue, blue eyes. His laugh, the feel of his breath against her skin. Her hand wrapped in his. He'd felt so real.

Beth shook her head now. "No. No, he was real." Her voice strengthened. "He *is* real. How could I lend a book to a ghost? How could I eat a pastry from a ghost?"

She looked at Jay, frowning, feeling a warm tear slide down her cheek.

"I have no idea," Jay admitted. "It doesn't make sense. None of this makes sense."

FOURTEEN

They didn't find much more information about Isaac. Beth looked up the history of the Lyttelton estate. Without a body, they'd had to wait years before the current Lord Lyttelton could be legally regarded as deceased. The estate had then passed to a cousin and dissolved eventually, as so many of the old-style households had at the time.

Beth continued to catch the same services to and from work. She decided not to change her departure time in the morning, in case the tram and its passengers miraculously reappeared. This was despite the angry driver's continuing behaviour. And the fact she could see no rails in the road.

Not long after the disappearance of the tram, Beth decided to check her friends weren't just catching a different service. Though why they would, she didn't know.

She took a day off work and caught the earliest service into town. She carried a clipboard and was prepared to tell anyone who asked she was doing some research into the public transport system. She'd even mocked up an ID card to show the drivers, in case they objected. She hoped she wouldn't get arrested for fraud.

Using a small fold-up stool she carried in with her to stand on, she looked into every bus passing by. For those with few passengers, she peered carefully at those inside to see if she spied anyone she knew.

With those having more passengers, she hopped on at the head of the queue and stood next to the driver to check those already on board as the new passengers got on. That way, she didn't hold them up.

No one bothered her much. She checked every single bus that passed through the main junction during the day and then on into the evening. The tram never pulled up and none of her friends appeared on any of the buses. No one even asked her for identification.

She boarded the last service home. It contained two men and a uniformed nurse she assumed was going home at the end of her shift. She and the nurse sat up the front.

Beth sat and stared at the window, looking at the mad woman facing her. Half of her face was yellow, half was in darkness, the lights of the city passing through it. She looked rather wild.

She hadn't even told Jay what she was doing. Beth had known it was insane.

She closed her eyes then and imagined she was sitting on the tram. The feel of the seats, the wooden poles, the silver and black painted swirls on the ceiling, the leather straps hanging down. The sound of the electricity humming through the overhead line. The clack of the doors. The *clang-clang!* of the bell as they got underway.

The first time she'd sat next to Isaac, she hadn't even spoken to him. He'd been looking out the window. Later, when she'd stood up for Tilly, he'd been smiling at her and they'd spoken then.

And the last time she'd see him? He'd been looking ill,

as had Willis. Had they known they wouldn't see her again? How?

She tried to imagine the sound of Isaac's voice and to conjure up his face in her mind. But the image was fuzzy.

Beth opened her eyes and retrieved her phone from her bag, switching it on after it being off all day. She wanted to look at his photo.

It took an age to start up. As several texts buzzed through from Jay—wondering where she was—she realised: yes, she missed Tilly and Margie and Willis, but in fact, it was all about Isaac.

His photo came up. Beth stared at him for a while and once more set it as her wallpaper. It wasn't the best of photos—it was a little out of focus and he wasn't smiling—but it was the only one she had that wasn't grainy and sepia-coloured.

Isaac! Where are you?

Beth bent her head down and tried to force the tears back. But they wouldn't go. She faced the window again—hiding. Out of the corner of her eye she'd seen the nurse look towards her.

This was something she couldn't explain to anyone except Jay.

When she got off she ran home, hoping Jay would be up. But she was already in bed, all the lights off bar the front porch. Not surprising—it was after midnight.

Beth confessed the next morning. But all Jay did was look at her and frown. Worried for her, probably. Understandable. Having an insane flatmate can't be good.

Week after week passed and nothing changed except the days got shorter and shorter.

Once a month had passed, Beth abandoned all hope. She

couldn't make the tram reappear and she would never see Isaac again. All the way to work and all the way back she brought up his photo on her phone and stared at it. She missed him.

Beth went over with Jay every little detail of the time she'd had with Isaac and re-examined it all with a fresh eye. A few things made more sense in the light of the new information. Jay listened and never judged; she was the best flatmate. In fact, she never said much at all. She must have been sick and tired of hearing about it by now.

Beth was lucky to have her not only as a flatmate, but as a friend.

She couldn't sleep and didn't want to eat. The computer research—at work and home—gave her a stiff neck. She couldn't concentrate and, a month later, Ruby had to give her a formal warning after a major mistake had several hundred new books put on the shelves with the same barcode printed on them. Beth had to go through the list, find the books, re-code them and re-shelve them all herself.

After this, Jay put her foot down and told Beth she had to visit a doctor, who diagnosed her with depression and prescribed some pills. It took some time for them to work. Beth felt dull-headed as a result.

Now Jay refused to hear any more about the tram—for Beth's own good, she said. So Beth stopped talking about it. The atmosphere at home became awkward.

The weather was getting colder, and Beth needed to buy that new winter coat. She recalled the day she'd splurged out on comfort food because Isaac had made it clear he wasn't interested. When in fact he was, but he'd been trying to pull away from her because he 'wasn't free'. The phrase had taken on whole new possibilities to Beth now.

She'd been able to save a substantial amount into the coat

fund envelope by this time.

Beth requested a week off work. She needed a break and the plan was to go and get a new coat from the factory shop on one of her days off.

"Do you want to come and help me pick it out?" she asked Jay. Beth admired Jay's style and knew she would help her get a good deal. And the time together might repair the strain that the friendship had endured.

"Yeah, absolutely," Jay replied, smiling.

At least Jay had actually seen Isaac and met Tilly and Margie. And Willis. That fact comforted Beth when she was tempted to believe herself crazy. But she was trying to put it all behind her.

They planned the day. As well as shopping, they were going to have lunch at a place in town near the factory shop mall. Jay offered to pay for lunch as she'd wanted to go to this particular restaurant for years.

Beth was happier than she'd been for a long time that morning, with plans ahead for time away from home with a good friend. Just a simple day out—a relaxing and easy day.

They hopped in the car after a late breakfast and drove to the other side of the city. Beth had her winter coat cash envelope stowed down in the bottom of her bag, waiting for the time it would be needed. She'd been researching on the internet for a while, and knew the type of coat she wanted. She had just enough money saved up.

The two women took their time and wandered from store to store, trying on different pieces of clothing as they went. Jay had a great eye and picked out some quirky items for both of them to experiment with. Not that Beth could buy any of them, but she needed to give different styles a go.

They walked to the restaurant in time for the reservation at noon. The food was delicious and Jay ordered wine, so they were merry indeed by the end of lunch. Beth's friendship with Jay was repairing. She felt lighter than she had in months.

Walking back to the mall afterwards, they went straight to the coat shop and trawled through the racks of coats in the seconds' section. They had many more coats than Beth had anticipated. After looking through them all, Jay called her over and showed her a coat she'd found. Beth tried it on. It fit.

Could it be that easy?

"Is it right, do you think?" she asked Jay—more than once.

"Yes. You look fabulous," she insisted. "Look in the mirror." She turned Beth around. "See how it's cinched in here? It's a flattering design. And a good length."

Jay stepped back and frowned then. "Gosh, Beth, you've lost weight, haven't you?"

Beth met her eyes in the mirror. "Yeah, probably. I haven't looked lately."

Jay put one of her arms around Beth's shoulders and squeezed, a wry smile on her face.

"I like the colour, too," added Beth. "It's not black or grey." It was a beautiful forest green.

"Shall we get it, then?" Jay asked.

Beth grinned. "Yes, let's. And I've got exactly the right amount for it." According to the price tag, anyway.

They took it up to the counter and asked the woman to ring it up. But when she told them the price, it wasn't what Beth was expecting.

"Are you sure?" she asked.

The woman beamed at her. "Yep. See the sign?" She pointed. "It's an extra ten per cent off. Today only."

"Fabulous," said Beth. "I'll have something left over." She pulled out her envelope and gave it to the woman, who paused at the sight of it.

"Cash. Oh goodness. I hope I've got the right change. Most

people don't use cash."

Beth sucked in a breath. "Is that going to be a problem?"

The woman shook her head. "Oh no. If all else fails, I'll pop next door and they'll have some. It might be lots of small change, though. I hope that's alright."

Relaxing, Beth nodded. "Yes, that's fine."

Beth waited for the change—the sales clerk did have to visit the store next door—while Jay took a call. By the time Jay returned, Beth had the coat in its carry-bag and was wondering what she would spend the leftover cash on.

But Jay looked worried. "My sister's little boy's had an accident. She needs to take him to hospital. I'll have to go over and take care of the other kids for a while. Sorry, we need to go now."

Beth frowned. "Doesn't your sister live in the other direction?"

Jay nodded.

"So why don't you go straight to her place and I'll make my own way home?" Beth could catch the bus. One to get to the bridge and then her usual one.

Jay looked at Beth, her head tilted. "Are you sure?"

"Yeah, absolutely. I've got lots of change." She waved her purse at her. "You go."

Beth could see Jay's whole body relaxing.

"Thank you. That's so helpful." Jay gave her a quick squeeze and began to walk out, then called back over her shoulder, "I'll see you later."

"Keep in touch," replied Beth.

———

Beth went on to visit the remaining stores in the mall. She didn't buy anything from them, however, as she'd already decided to buy a scarf she'd seen in town. The one thing she did get was an ice cream as a treat before the long trek home. She sat next to the food hall's fountain to eat it, watching the people, their voices ringing off the overhead glass dome.

The mall had its own bus stop and Beth sat down to wait. The bus arrived and began its circuitous journey to the bridge. Beth found herself a comfortable seat and settled in for the long haul.

She wasn't familiar with the area she had to get off in and, though she'd asked for directions from the driver, she got lost. She had to stop again to ask somebody else. She'd missed a turn.

Doubling back, she'd walked into one particular street when she saw three figures up ahead. They immediately turned off onto the next road, walking out of her sight.

But, in those few moments, Beth recognised them.

It was the bullyboys.

Beth ran. She was breathless when she reached the corner. She peered around it.

The boys were crossing the road halfway along. One was shoving another and all of them were talking and laughing in their familiar, taunting way. They'd found a can and were kicking it about the place between them.

Some trees had been planted along this road, and Beth ran from one to the next, trying to make sure the boys didn't see her. She wasn't sure why she was doing this, but it felt like the right thing to do. They were the only connection to the tram she'd come across since Isaac had gone missing. She didn't want to lose them.

From behind one tree, she watched one of the boys deliberately kick the can at the side of a car and then lean over to look at the result. When he pointed, his mates laughed and both of them lined the can up and copied him, each trying to make the biggest mark.

They were stopped only by the sudden appearance of a man coming out of a building nearby. They walked away, whistling, and rounded the next corner.

Beth ran again. The boys were now sitting on the seat at a bus stop—the stop she'd been looking for.

What should she do? Stand where she was until the tram rolled up? No, the stop was too far away; it would leave without her. Go and wait with them?

She realised she was assuming the tram would come to pick them up. That was insane. Why should it?

Beth now brought to the front of her mind the fantastical theory she'd been dismissing for months: Isaac was a prisoner on a magical tram and the boys were his jailers. They were the only passengers from the end of the line she'd seen get on and off. Perhaps the others couldn't.

Crazy though it was, she had to try the theory out. If she was right, it would be the tram picking them up and she would be able to get on, too. If she was wrong, she would get her bus home and that would be that.

So she straightened, and walked around the corner and up to the stop. She was behind the boys so they didn't see her as they were jabbing each other and giggling.

She stood and waited, studying them.

They were all no more than twelve or thirteen, she guessed. Perhaps a little older. They wore school uniforms: grey, half-untucked shirts and dark blue shorts. Their long socks had a dark blue stripe at the top, though most were sagging around their ankles. They also wore caps. Each of them had a satchel or a small backpack.

The longer they sat there, the rougher their antics got, until one of them was pushed off the end of the seat. The other two collapsed in laughter.

Complaining, the boy who'd fallen jumped to his feet,

ready to belt them. But he stopped when he saw Beth. His hands fell to his sides and he glared at her, jaw clenched. Beth's chest constricted as she remembered: she'd thrown their friend off the tram, and she hadn't seen him since.

This boy was tall and lanky, his hair a greasy dark brown.

Three young men and one woman, in an industrial area with no one around and the sun beginning to set.

Perhaps this wasn't such a good idea after all.

His reaction alerted the other two to her presence and they, too, stood and circled around the bench, glaring at her.

She had to remain calm.

"What are you doing here?" sneered one of them. He was the shortest and was tubby with a shock of matted blonde hair.

Beth raised her eyebrow. "Catching the bus," she replied. Wanting to push it a little further, she added, "Do I know you?" She looked at the third boy. He had tight, red curls and his face was covered in freckles.

He glanced at the others, uncertain now. "No." His reply was stroppy.

She looked around at the three of them. "Well, nice to meet you. I'm Beth."

Tallboy stalked over to her. "What have you got in the bag?" He stopped right in front of her—way too close—and pushed his face towards her.

Would they attack her?

"A winter coat. In fact," she added—she had a sudden idea. "It's pretty cold, isn't it?"

She lifted the bag up between them and reached in. Pulling the coat out in one move, she thrust the bag at him.

"Hold this for me, will you?" she said.

Startled, he took it and Beth shook the coat out and put it on.

"What do you think?" she asked, posing for them.

"You're a freak! I don't want this." Tallboy retreated and threw the bag back at her. At least that had got him further away from her. She picked it up.

But now the other boys stepped up.

"You look stupid. You're so fat."

"Ew, you're ugly." This boy flung his finger at her, stopping short of touching her face. "See, she's all sweaty. Sweaty pig!" He yelled this in her face, making her jump back. They laughed.

"Well push off, then, you ugly, sweaty pig," said Tallboy, recovering his composure as his friends backed him up.

They hadn't touched her. She wondered if they could.

"No. I'm staying right here." Beth kept her voice as quiet and even as she could.

The three of them set themselves up in a semicircle around her then, with her back against the wall, and looked her up and down. Tallboy spread his legs wide and folded his arms. They were all right up in her face.

"You're small for a girl," said Freckles.

They're trying to scare me.

She didn't bother responding. But they kept trying, each comment or question increasingly explicit and more and more disturbing. They tried every disgusting word or gesture Beth had heard of, and some she hadn't. Some made her skin crawl.

But in the end it got so ridiculous, Beth laughed. That really riled them up. But their shouting tantrums were interrupted by the arrival of the bus. At this, they sauntered away in different directions, leaving the way open for her to board.

She didn't.

The bus driver leaned towards her and yelled, "Are you getting on?"

Beth shook her head and called back, "No, thank you. I'm waiting for the next one."

The driver frowned and, looking back and forth at the boys on either side of the stop, shook his head in disbelief. "You sure?"

She waved at him and smiled. "Yes, thanks."

They hadn't touched her yet. Beth was betting they wouldn't—a high stakes wager.

The bus drove away. The circling boys returned.

"Why didn't you get on?" asked Tubby.

Beth smiled at him. "I don't want to be too early, do I?"

They tried shouting at her, all at once, screaming filthy words and threats, but she folded her arms and weathered the storm. She was beginning to believe all they could do was make noise at her.

The boys eventually gave up and walked away together to confer in a group on one side.

Her feet were hurting from all the shopping so she decided to sit down while she had the chance. As she did, she checked the timetable on the post.

Only one more bus left to come. The rest didn't pass through this area—it was only used during the day. She'd have to walk for over an hour to get back on the route.

Beth wondered why the boys didn't just go to another stop. Did they only use certain ones, or did they have to use a particular stop once they'd arrived? She had no way of knowing.

And what would she do if they left?

She would follow them.

Was she mad? If Isaac—a full-grown man—was nervous of them, she had no chance. Why was she doing this? Did she truly believe some sort of magic had Isaac trapped? Wasn't that simply ridiculous?

Whether he was trapped or not, Beth wanted so badly to see Isaac she was prepared to risk it.

That tram had better come.

Her phone pinged.

JAY: Need a lift?

Beth declined the offer. It was too risky to have someone else around.

Now, assuming this ridiculous theory was true, she ran again through all the many trips she'd enjoyed on the tram and made some surprising discoveries.

She'd never—not once—had to travel on a bus. Whenever she'd needed transport the tram had arrived and taken her where she wanted to go. She also decided she hadn't been imagining things when she'd been late to catch it and had still been able to get on board. It had been late *for her.* Even when she'd had to go home from work early, the tram had changed its normal time and come to take her home. She recalled she'd even thought she'd seen Isaac on that trip, too. Had he been hiding so she wouldn't suspect?

The theory made her sound extraordinarily self-absorbed, which was partly why she'd dismissed it—up until now. How could she be at the centre of this strange mystery? What did any of this have to do with her?

And yet this one thing pulled all the threads together.

Beth wasn't able to remember if everyone had always been on board the tram every time. For a start, she hadn't known them all from the beginning. She could only recall seeing Maxine on board twice for sure, but that didn't mean she hadn't been sitting up the back somewhere. To be honest, she'd only had eyes for Isaac. She couldn't even remember if the bullies had got on every time.

Someone sat down next to Beth.

It wasn't one of the boys. It was a man and he was sitting far closer than he had to. She hadn't even heard him coming.

By rights she should have smelled him coming—he reeked of booze. Where had he been drinking around here?

Beth looked about her for the boys. They were leaning against the wall a little way away and smirking as they watched her.

The man was looking directly at her. "Hello, love," he drawled. He leaned closer. Beth could hear the boys sniggering.

She put on a cheery voice. "Hello, sir. How are you this evening?" She was being a bit loud, too. Was it bravado? Because this was a real man and he was a real threat. He sat up a little, startled.

"I'm..." he trailed off, staring down her body. He started again. "You pretty." He was almost drooling on her. Lord, his breath stank.

"Well, thank you very much." She was still being loud. "Because those young men over there were being less than complimentary before." She pointed at the boys on the off chance their presence would make the man behave better. "They told me I was ugly."

"What? Thaz rude!" He looked at them. "You got no taste, boys. This here's a bootiful woman." He turned back to her and the lean came on him again. "Very, very bootiful." His voice became quiet. "Hey, baby. Ya wanna come out wiv me?" He smiled widely, forgetting to pull his tongue back into his mouth.

Beth nearly laughed, but stopped herself just in time. That was likely to anger him.

"What a kind offer, thank you! But I'm afraid..." She put her hand on his shoulder to straighten him up—he was about to fall on her. "I'm sorry, but I have an important meeting tonight. I'm speaking for them and I can't let them down."

She looked at her watch. "I do hope…" Thinking about what she was about to say, she changed her mind.

He'll expect to catch the bus with me, if I say that.

She picked up where she'd left off, after a brief—hopefully not too suspicious—pause. "I do hope my friend isn't late picking me up."

The last bus was due any moment now.

Wanting to take control of the conversation, she asked him, "So, what do you do for a living?"

The man made a face. "Aaggh. I'm a machinist. Over there." He pointed to an enormous building along the street with the name 'Quigley's' emblazoned on the front wall.

"A machinist. What does a machinist do?" she asked.

Just keep him occupied until the bus comes.

He held up a hand. "Oh, thaz boring." His face projected towards Beth. "What do you do?" he said. Here came the lean again.

Beth's hand whipped up to his shoulder. "I'm a librarian. I love books. Do you like books?" Still a bit loud.

The man sighed. "Not really."

Beth spotted the bus approaching. "Well, here's the last bus. See you again, eh?"

"Yeeaapp," he said.

The bus pulled up to the stop and the man stood up—mostly. One of his knees didn't cooperate and he had to use his hands to straighten it.

But then he swung around. "Hey, whas ya phone nummer?"

Beth froze. After what felt like a long moment, she felt something in her new coat's pocket. She pulled the label card out and gave it to him, making sure she didn't look at it. "Here you are. Better hurry."

He grinned, clutching his new treasure, and stumbled

aboard.

The driver was looking impatient—and miffed he had a drunk getting on. But he didn't close the door straight away.

"Are you gonna be okay?" he asked Beth.

"Yes, I'm fine," she reassured him.

He glanced behind her. "This is the last service through here. Are you sure?"

"Yes. I'm sure. Thank you." She waved him on as confidently as she could manage.

He gave her a doubtful look, then shrugged, closed the door and drove away.

She went to sit down again and found the boys right in her face. They were not impressed.

"Whadaya think ya doin'?" Freckles' face was close.

"Well, boys..." She folded her arms. "I'm concerned about you."

Their jaws dropped in unison. "What?"

"You're minors. I have a responsibility to make sure you're going to be okay," she explained.

"We'll be fine, ya silly cow, when you go away and leave us alone," yelled Tallboy.

"Oh, no," said Beth, "I insist. I won't leave here until you boys have all been picked up by your parents." She pointed at the sky. "It's dark now. I can't leave you here in the dark. It's not safe."

They stared at her. Then Tubby grabbed the elbows of the other two and dragged them away to a point out of her hearing.

The boys stood in a huddle having a serious discussion Beth couldn't hear a word of. In the meantime, she sat down again to wait.

What would they do?

Her phone rang.

"Where are you?" Jay's voice was tense. "I just got home and you're not here."

"I'm…" Beth said and then looked around her. Jay wasn't going to be happy about this. But, because she was such a good friend, Beth would tell her anyway.

She spoke clearly. "I'm about to catch the tram again."

"What?" Jay's voice was breathless and high.

"I'm catching the tram." Beth made her voice as reassuring as she could. "Jay, I'm going to see Isaac again. But if I don't come back, see if you can find the bullyboys. They're the only ones who can get off and on. I've been following them. They're the key to—"

Her phone cut out with a loud crackle. She looked at it. The screen was black and she couldn't make it light up at all.

How did that happen?

She heard one of the boys huff and then they were standing in front of her. Tallboy spoke for them. "Well, lady, if that's what you want." He leaned forward. "But I hope you know what you're getting into."

The three of them smiled knowingly down at her and then paraded away.

Did she? Did she know what she was getting into? Wasn't she walking into a world where she didn't know the rules? Couldn't she easily get trapped herself?

She could get up now and walk away; that was the other option. And then what would happen? She would never see these boys again and she would most certainly never see Isaac again.

Isaac. He was worth the risk, wasn't he? So were Tilly, Willis and Margie. Could it be those people were depending on her to get them out of this?

Could she get them out? She had no idea.

But she had to try, damn it. She was going to try.

—— FIFTEEN ——

First she heard the zing of the electricity through the line, then the familiar sound of the wheels on the tracks. The tracks that weren't there.

The tram materialised out of a mist, cruising its way towards her. She could see Willis in the driver's seat. Tilly and Margie sat together halfway down, Gareth opposite. And Maxine sat in the second-to-last row, staring out the window. But it was too dark for them to see her.

Beth found herself on her feet, holding her breath. She didn't even remember standing up.

Isaac—her Isaac—sat in his usual seat, behind the back door. His head was bowed down. Beth's heart leapt at the sight of him. She would take hold of him and never let go!

And then the bullyboys were standing in front of her. They wanted to be first on so they stood between her and Willis as the doors clacked open.

Little Masters Tubby and Freckles hurled themselves up the steps and pounded down the aisle, but Tallboy climbed the stairs and stood and stared at Willis for a moment before stalking to the back.

Willis was wide-eyed and pale as a result. What had the boy done? Beth hadn't heard him say anything.

Beth stepped up into the tram and waited for Willis to recognise her.

She couldn't tell when his wide eyes changed from fear to amazement, but he opened his mouth as she put her fare in the little wooden bowl.

"Dear Beth. Is that you, love?" His voice was shaking and small. In the meantime, his hands automatically scooped up and distributed the coins into their sections in the box and then handed Beth's ticket to her. Did he have a choice in doing that? His hands seemed unconnected to his conscious will.

"Hello, my friend. It's so good to see you again." Beth's voice wavered and she could barely keep her tears contained. She pulled aside his driver's barrier and wrapped her arms around him. He hugged her back.

When she straightened, she saw someone in the corner of her eye. Gareth was half standing in his seat, eyes wide, jaw slack.

Gareth's obvious excitement in turn piqued the curiosity of Tilly and Margie who gasped at the sight of Beth. They jumped up and bustled forward, Tilly calling over her shoulder, "M'lord!"

Beth found herself wrapped in the arms of two weeping women, kissing her ferociously on her cheeks and stroking her hair.

"My goodness, you've lost weight, Beth dear! Have a pastry." Margie picked up her basket, which she'd discarded onto a nearby seat.

But Tilly took Beth's face in her hands. "What are you doing here?" she whispered, her face full of fear—a fear that Beth realised was for her.

Beth smiled for Tilly, fighting to be brave. "I forced my way on, Tilly. I saw the boys and followed them."

She turned to indicate the boys in the back seat, but found Isaac standing before her. Beth was transfixed by him.

Tilly stepped out of the way.

Isaac's eyes were full of an intensity Beth hadn't seen in them before.

"Elizabeth." His voice was cracked and rough. "I have missed you."

Beth reached forward and took his hand. He held on fast and pulled her to him, wrapping his arms around her and settling her head in under his chin. She felt him breathing into her hair as he cupped his hand around the back of her head.

She revelled in his embrace, feeling the warmth of his body against hers. He was definitely real. She could hear his heart beating. He was alive. She wanted to stay like this forever, but at that point the tram surged forward and they were on their way.

Beth looked up at him. "How can I get you off here?"

The little joy in his face drained away, but he said nothing.

Beth clutched at him and shook him. "How do I get you off this tram?"

Isaac's eyes widened and he took a sudden breath in. His arms fell to his sides as he straightened and became rigid.

"Isaac! What's happening?" Something about this felt familiar to Beth.

A mocking voice rang out: *"Oh, Elizabeth, my darling, I missed you so much!"*

Tallboy, halfway down the aisle, was addressing Freckles, who clasped his hands together at his chest and put on a falsetto.

"Isaac, my Isaac. Come to me."

The two boys flounced about and then embraced each

other, making ridiculous noises in their mockery.

In the meantime, Isaac relaxed, though he took a trembling breath and held the nearest seat for support. Beth ignored the boys and moved close to Isaac.

"They did that to you, didn't they?" she whispered.

His head down, Isaac didn't answer either way, and Beth suspected he couldn't answer, or would suffer if he did.

Gareth stepped up. "Let's all sit down, shall we?" Maxine was standing behind him.

The six of them—Tilly, Margie, Gareth, Maxine, Isaac and Beth—perched on the aisle end of three rows of seats right at the front of the tram, so Willis could listen in, too.

Gareth began. "It's a lovely surprise to see you again, Beth." All the others nodded enthusiastically. Even Maxine.

Beth smiled at him. "Thank you. I thought I'd never see any of you again, but I saw the boys on the road and followed them to a stop." She could see the boys prowling at the back of the tram, staring at her with animosity. They whispered amongst themselves.

Her friends remained silent and her suspicion they were being controlled grew stronger.

Well then, she would do the talking.

"I've done some research," she said, looking around at them all. "I found out who you all are and where and when you came from."

All their eyes were fixed on her as she continued, pointing at Isaac. "You're Lord Isaac Gordon Francis Lyttelton." He huffed in surprise as she indicated Maxine. "You're Lady Maxine Mandeville, and the rest of you worked for Isaac, on his estate in England."

As Beth searched Isaac's face, she detected an air of admiration. She reached out and took his hand in hers.

"You all went missing over a hundred years ago," she

continued. "None of you have aged. You all wear the same clothes every day." She'd just noticed that.

Beth sighed. "I need to figure out how to get you off. You don't seem to be able to tell me anything, or even indicate if I'm right." It seemed the more she knew, the harder it became to find out more.

Is that what had happened? She'd figured something out—even if she hadn't realised it at the time—and the boys had stopped her coming on board? Was that what the antique coins had been all about?

She'd only got here by accident then. If she hadn't spotted and followed the boys, she would never have seen her friends again. That was why they were so surprised to see her.

The boys wouldn't let it happen again.

She looked around at her friends. "This is my last chance, isn't it? If I don't figure out how to get you off, you'll disappear forever and I'll never get another chance."

Still no response. Beth frowned. This was going to be difficult.

The tram stopped and Beth looked out the window. They were at the depot.

Diesels didn't come here. This was where Beth had heard that eerie scream. And Jay had had a sudden attack of amnesia— or blindness. Why did it seem like Beth was the only one who could see this place? What was so special about it?

Beth stood up. "I wonder if I'll find any clues around here." But Isaac tightened his grip. His hold was so firm it became painful. He stared at her and his face was pale. He was afraid of something.

Beth got the message. "It's okay, I won't go outside." Willis had been able to state this as a rule before, she remembered.

"I'll stay on the tram. I promise." She placed her other hand on the side of Isaac's face, bending down to look him in the eye.

He let go, but rose and followed her to the front door. Willis had already got off and was turning the tram. Beth descended the first couple of steps and found Isaac's hand on her shoulder, preventing her going any further.

She was surprised he was allowed to do this much.

As she stood on the steps, she heard sounds that made her shrink back. Again, the shriek, almost like a fox. And the longer she remained the more she heard: indistinct keening and deep, bone-juddering moans emerged from unseen mouths hidden in the darkness outside. They hinted at an evil she had no way of identifying.

The only light was from the tram itself, and that didn't reach far. She couldn't even see the other trams. The all-consuming darkness suggested an eternal space full of less-than nothing. Of hunger and regret. Of depths of need that could never be filled. The tram was a small pool of light in the midst of it.

Willis returned to the tram and gasped when he found Beth standing just inside the door.

She asked, "Do you hear those sounds every time you come out?"

For a moment, it looked like Willis was going to reply, but she saw him stiffen and his jaw clamp shut as he marched—or was marched—back up the steps.

She was getting a clearer picture now: some things they could say, some they couldn't. But even if she understood that much, it was still a puzzle.

She'd heard a scream when she'd thrown the bullyboy off the tram for swearing at Tilly all those weeks ago. She was surprised she'd been able to shrug it off so easily. These sounds frightened her to the very core of her being.

I never saw that boy again.

The back of her neck prickled.

Isaac shifted his grip down to her elbow and pulled Beth away from the door. It closed and once more they were on the move.

Was the hungry darkness—whatever it was—responsible for what had happened to her friends?

How long did she have to figure this out? Until the end of the line, she presumed. Not long for a puzzle with no clues. She was certain that, if she got off now, the tram and its passengers would be moved farther away from her and she would never find them again.

Beth and Isaac sat down again amidst the others. Beth reached out to hold Isaac's hand. He took hers in both of his and kissed it, his eyes closed.

I have to save him!

"I don't feel like I've got many clues," she whispered.

The boys cackled from the back of the tram.

Beth looked at Isaac, frowning. "Can they hear us?"

His sombre look was the only confirmation she was to get. She remembered the multitude of times the bullyboys' laughter had erupted, seemingly at what had been said, though they couldn't possibly have heard. And her friends' reactions at the time—though muted—had hinted the same.

Beth would have to assume they could hear everything on the tram. It would make this nigh impossible.

Beth looked around at the faces of her friends. Every one of them was devoid of hope. Even if they could communicate with her, perhaps they couldn't tell her anything anyway.

Tilly was opposite her and she reached out, smiling. "It's been such a delight getting to know you, dear. You've brought us such joy. I'll remember this always."

She's saying goodbye!

This was more than disturbing. Beth wasn't ready to say

goodbye. She looked away and saw through the windows where they were. An alarm went off in her head.

"Wait a minute! We're much closer to my stop than we should be."

The boys cackled at this, and advanced up the aisle towards the group.

Beth stood up, defensive.

"There's nothing you can do," said Freckles in a sing-song voice.

"They're ours. You can't take them away. Loser!" said Tubby.

They weren't even trying to hide the reality of the situation now. They were feeling confident.

Tallboy was the one putting on a falsetto voice now. *"Oh, my only love!"* He had a languid hand on his chest. *"I must leave you behind and never see you again."* He ended his performance with a burst of fake weeping that transformed into loud laughter.

Isaac squeezed her hand.

The tram was passing Beth's stop now. She didn't have much time.

The three boys were standing among the group now, bending down and laughing in her friends' faces, mocking them as they held them in their control. Beth couldn't bear it.

She raised her voice. "Oh, shut up, you lot! Or I'll throw you off."

Now it was the boys' turn to freeze. Their laughter stopped, they looked towards her and the look was nervous.

Ah! So I can do that, can I?

But what would that achieve? Her friends would still be stuck on board.

The boys, however, skipped out of her reach, further down the back of the tram. And they stopped the taunting.

Beth said to Isaac, "If I threw them off, would they still be able to control you?"

Of course, he couldn't give an answer, but one came nevertheless—from the boys: "Yes, of course we can. Ha ha!" Tallboy yelled at her.

Releasing Isaac's hand, Beth advanced on him, her fists clenched. "Oh, let's give it a try, eh? It wouldn't hurt to try."

The boys scuttled out of her reach as she chased them about. They were fast, leaping over and under the seats, sliding about on the floor, giggling and mocking her.

She was thinking of giving up when she found herself surrounded by the three of them. They were grinning manically, none of them out of breath. Tubby and Freckles were between her and her friends. She was facing Tallboy at the back of the Tram.

Why had they stopped running?

She reached for his ear and heard a cry of alarm behind her. "Beth!"

As her hand flew towards him, Tallboy's face distorted, his skin split apart into shreds to reveal stained bone beneath, the rotting eyes staring, lidless, back at her. When the face opened its maw, she saw a darkness within matching the darkness she'd seen in the depot. It was the void of the grave—the hunger that's never filled.

Eerily, the same young boy's voice came out of that pit of despair. "Final stop!" it cried.

The tram had indeed stopped.

Beth had retracted her hand in horror by now as she stared at the gruesome creature before her. A slimy eel of a tongue emerged to taunt her.

She spun around and found two more revolting brutes behind her. She was surrounded.

But being trapped simply angered Beth further and she yelled at what was once Tallboy. "I can still throw you off, kid!"

She had the satisfaction of seeing him shrink back from her, which confirmed it. Yes, she could throw him off. And they still couldn't touch her?

Once he found her undaunted by his grotesque form, he reassumed the shape of the tall, skinny boy as before. Easier to get around, perhaps. But he was still pressed up against the back wall.

Beth gritted her teeth and reached for his ear.

She almost had it when he threw up his arms and cried, "Don't!"

She drew back. "Okay." She assumed a voice of reason. "I won't throw you off—if you'll let them go."

A laugh of disbelief exploded from him. "I can't do that."

Beth's hand darted forward and grabbed his ear. "Right, then." She pulled him towards the nearest door. Their ears were their weakest point, it seemed.

Tallboy talked fast, his voice high. "I really, really can't let them go. I don't have that kind of power. Please, believe me!" He tried to struggle as he talked, but he couldn't get loose. They were at the door.

"Wait, wait!" he cried. "There is something I can do."

Beth stopped. "What?" She had no patience with this.

He looked up at her sidelong, wincing in her grip. "We'll let them talk and do what they want. You can ask them questions and they'll be able to answer. We can do that, can't we boys?" He waved encouragement to his cohorts from his bent-over position.

Tubby and Freckles had let Beth pass them and were now as far down the aisle from her as they could get. But they nodded and agreed from where they were. "Yeah, yeah, we can do that," they chorused, nodding.

Beth let go of Tallboy's ear and took hold of the front of his shirt at the same time, pulling his face up to hers. "You get down the back. If I can't get the answers I want, I will come and get you." And she shoved him away.

He scurried up the back as she spun around to search her friends' faces.

"Are you free? Can you talk?"

She watched as they relaxed and nodded at her. Willis stood and joined them.

"Beth, love, you haven't got much time," he warned her.

"How much?" she asked.

He looked at his watch. "Seven minutes… seven and a half minutes on the timetable."

Something else then made sense to Beth. "And then the doors will close and it'll drive away by itself? Like it did when I tried to visit the end of the line?"

Willis nodded.

And then Beth realised something else. "And that was why you were so mean to me, Isaac—you had to get me off." She made another connection. "Will I be trapped on here, if I stay?"

They all nodded at her: "Yes." The urgency in their eyes told her that was not something she wanted.

"But why—"

But Isaac had already anticipated her question. "It was my foolish pride that got us stuck here in the first place. But never mind—there's no time to explain. It's *our* fate, Beth, not *yours*."

"No!" She couldn't just give up. "I won't leave you. Tell me what I need to know to get you off."

But once again came the silence she'd come to dread as she looked from face to face. She swung around and glared at the boys in the back of the tram. They held up their hands, trying to look innocent.

Then Tilly said, "No, Beth. We're free to speak."

Tilly held her hands out to her, empty, and went on. "But we don't know the answers, dear. We've been trying to solve this since the beginning." She sighed. "Oh, so long ago."

Isaac spoke again. "It's a mystery to us too, Beth. We don't know. We simply don't know. We got on this blasted tram—it was my idea, I led them all here!—and we've never been able to get off."

"Don't say that!" Beth protested. Her heart broke at the despair on Isaac's face. "You can't tell me there's nothing I can do. You can't!" Tears brimmed in her eyes.

Isaac came to her then and wrapped her in his arms. "Oh, dear Beth. I'm so sorry." He buried his face in her hair and whispered, "All we can do is say goodbye."

He'd given up.

But Beth couldn't—not yet. She'd only just found him!

She ranted against his chest. "Magic! I thought magic was supposed to be fun." She raged through her tears.

She felt other hands patting her back as well as Isaac's warm embrace, his heart beating against her ear.

She opened her eyes.

Magic.

The word had given her an idea. It had worked in the stories.

Well, it's worth a try. What have I got to lose?

She tipped her head back and threw her hands around the back of Isaac's head. Pulling his startled face down to hers, she kissed him. Yes, they were just fairy tales, but why not give it a try—see if love really could work its magic?

But Isaac was not a reluctant participant. After the first gasp of shock, he pressed his lips to hers. One hand slid around the nape of her neck, the other splayed across her lower back and he pulled her body up against his.

This experiment soon found both of them abandoned to

the fullness of their emotions. Absorbed in the sensuality of the kiss, Beth relished every touch of lip or teeth or tongue. She wanted to remember it all.

In case it didn't work.

They finally broke off and dwelt momentarily in the afterglow, foreheads pressed together.

Beth had to force herself away to pull Isaac to the front door of the tram.

"See if you can get off," she commanded him.

Though he now realised her intent, Isaac's face held little hope for success. But he gave her a smile and dutifully tried to step down onto the pavement.

His foot could not leave the bottom step. He was constrained by an invisible barrier. He even lifted his arms and pressed his entire bodyweight against what looked like empty air. After a few attempts, he faced Beth again, his eyes lowered. He seemed to have been expecting nothing more.

"Beth," Willis spoke. "You haven't much time left, love." He spoke to Isaac. "M'lord, I suggest you stay on the steps. If time gets too short, you may need to throw her off."

Isaac nodded.

Though Beth was stunned with disappointment, her friends then crowded her.

Tilly came first. She put her arms around her and hugged her. "Have a wonderful life, my dear." Her head was bowed as she turned away, tears in her eyes.

Margie came next. "You're a sweet girl, Beth." She hugged her, too. "You'll remember us, won't ye?" She sniffled as she offered Beth a last selection of pastries. But this time Beth declined; she was most definitely not hungry.

Gareth shook Beth's hand, his hand still wrapped in its bandage. "You are quite a whirlwind of a woman, Beth. I'm glad to have met you. I wish we'd spoken more." He dipped his head in a small bow.

Maxine shook her hand, too, her tiny hands encased in gloves. "Thank you for trying. Please forgive me for being mean to you. I meant only to help."

Once each of them had said their goodbye, they took a seat again on the tram, resigned to their eternal prison.

Willis gave her a quick hug. "You're a magnificent woman, Beth." He settled himself back in the driver's seat, his head inclined away from her.

She leaned over the barrier and gave him a peck on the cheek, which put a bashful smile on his face before he spoke again.

"Not long now," he said. "Be ready, m'lord."

To throw her off, he meant. Beth's mind raced.

She looked around for an emergency exit. She could see none. Could she smash a window? She doubted that would work. Willis' window opened, but surely they would have tried that.

As her eyes played over the rest of the driver's area, the tickets and the cash-box, Willis' frequent phrase echoed in her mind: *Can't let you off until you've paid your fare.*

Which gave her an idea. A desperate, crazy, stupid idea. But it was all she had.

"Willis, give me a ticket to the end of the line, please," she said, getting her purse out.

Automatically, it seemed, he reached for the metal keys and a fare amount came up as his eyebrows rose.

It couldn't be that simple, could it?

She put the cash required in the wooden bowl and Willis, blinking, handed her a ticket.

Maxine had sat down in the single seat opposite the driver. Beth gave her the ticket and gestured for her to get off the tram.

Maxine paused for a moment and then, shrugging, stood and made her way down the steps—all the way to the ground. Her eyes as big as saucers, she looked up at Isaac. He, in turn, looked around at Beth, his face taut.

Beth spoke to Willis again. "Give me another ticket to the end of the line, please, Willis." She couldn't speak fast enough.

Once again, Willis rang up the fare, collected the cash Beth put in the bowl and gave her a ticket.

By this time, Gareth, Tilly and Margie had jumped up again and were waiting in a bunch at the end of the aisle.

Tilly got the next ticket and Isaac and Maxine assisted her to the ground, though Isaac was hampered by the invisible barrier.

Margie was next and then Gareth. The tension was palpable as the next ticket was purchased. Beth held it out to Isaac but he refused it.

"No, give it to Willis," he said.

But Beth wasn't having that and she spoke with some heat in her voice. "Don't argue with me. We haven't got time. Get off!"

But Isaac shook his head, his jaw set. "I will not get off until everyone else is free."

Beth wondered at his resolve, admired it—even as it pained her to hear him utter those words. He'd borne this responsibility for over a hundred years. She couldn't imagine the guilt he felt.

Willis jumped out of his seat, took the ticket and stepped down to the ground. He then took Isaac's place on the lowest step as Isaac sat in the driver's chair. Willis would pull Beth off if time ran out.

Would it work with Isaac in the driver's chair, though?

The bullyboys had made their way to this end of the aisle by now and were staring at the proceedings, their eyes bulging.

It seemed they couldn't do a thing about it.

"Another ticket to the end of the line, please." Beth threw the rest of her change into the wooden bowl.

But Isaac didn't do anything.

She swung around. "It doesn't work for him. Willis…"

But Willis interrupted. "There's not enough, Beth," he said. His face was pale.

Beth didn't have enough money. Her stomach sank through the bottom of her feet.

She shouldn't have had the ice cream. How could she live with herself? Isaac would be trapped on here all by himself.

"I'll stay, too," she said impulsively, but saw the two men exchange a look and felt Willis take hold of her waist.

NO!

"Willis, how much time?" Isaac asked.

"Just over a minute."

"Oh, no! Isaac!" Beth cried. She frantically searched the bottom of her bag for any hint of loose change that might have hidden itself.

She found nothing.

Tilly called up the steps. "Could this help? I collected these when I found them on the floor."

She held out a handkerchief tied in a knot. As Beth took it, she felt a hard bundle within—a few small coins.

Her hands shook as she struggled with the knot and tried to count the coins. But some of them were so old and worn, she couldn't tell how much they were worth. Throwing everything into the wooden bowl, she stopped and looked at Isaac, hoping beyond hope. Willis took a firmer hold of her.

Several terrifyingly long seconds passed.

But Isaac's hands reached out abruptly and issued the ticket, distributing the coins into their places. He stood up from the driver's chair, Beth grabbed his arm and the three of them raced down the stairs to freedom.

"But, what about us? Pay for us, too!" The bullyboys were on the steps now, chins trembling. "We haven't got a driver. What are we going to do?"

Isaac stared up at them. Beth could see he was torn. He looked at the ticket in his hand and her heart seized in alarm.

"Isaac," she said, pulling him around, her voice urgent, "you're not responsible for them. Whatever fault you bore, you've more than paid your debt." She shook his arm. "Those creatures do not belong in this world."

As he took in her words, his face cleared and he nodded.

He turned back to the boys. "You've got your bus passes. You can take care of yourselves." He wrapped his arms around Beth and stepped back from the tram, pulling her with him.

With a hiss and a clack, the door shut on the horrified boys. The tram *clang-clang*'ed merrily and rolled away down the road into the darkness, no one in the driver's seat.

The last they saw was the bullies' faces pressed against the back window, as the tram dissolved into the mist.

The seven of them stood on the pavement there in the night and looked at one another. So quiet. No rumbling of rails beneath them.

"Look... stars!" whispered Tilly. She tilted her head back. Her eyes were wide.

Willis was looking up too. "So bright," he murmured.

Beth felt Isaac's warm hand encircle hers. His eyes shone in the streetlight as he smiled.

Making my acquaintance...

Beth's heart fluttered.

"So, my love," he said. "Where to from here?"

FREE DOWNLOAD

Sign up for the author's New Releases mailing list
and get a free short story.

Go here to get started: susanholt.nz/free

IF YOU ENJOYED
THIS BOOK...

please help me out by leaving an honest review
on Amazon at myBook.to/CtLT

And if you're feeling extra generous, please look
me up on Goodreads, too.

Thank you so much! We authors are completely
reliant on you wonderful readers, so keep
enjoying stories and I'll see you in the next book...